Look for these titles by
Dana Marie Bell

Now Available:

Halle Pumas Series
The Wallflower
Sweet Dreams
Cat of a Different Color
Steel Beauty
Only in My Dreams

Halle Shifters Series
Bear Necessities
Cynful

True Destiny Series
Very Much Alive
Eye of the Beholder
Howl for Me

The Gray Court Series
Dare to Believe
Noble Blood
Artistic Vision

Poconos Pack Series
Finding Forgiveness

Heart's Desire Series
Shadow of the Wolf
Hecate's Own

Print Anthologies
Hunting Love
Mating Games
Animal Attraction

Praise for *Artistic Vision*

"When this dragon and sidhe come together fire is the least of their worries."
~ *Sizzling Hot Book Reviews*

"This is a great story woven by a storyteller who knows just how much to reveal and how much to hold back..."
~ *Manic Readers Review Depot*

"The characters have such vivid personalities, I expected to look up and see them materialize in front of me."
~ *Night Owl Reviews*

Artistic Vision

Dana Marie Bell

Samhain Publishing, Ltd.
11821 Mason Montgomery Road, 4B
Cincinnati, OH 45249
www.samhainpublishing.com

Artistic Vision
Copyright © 2012 by Dana Marie Bell
Print ISBN: 978-1-60928-790-0
Digital ISBN: 978-1-60928-553-1

Editing by Tera Kleinfelter
Cover by Kendra Egert

This book is a work of fiction. The names, characters, places, and incidents are products of the writer's imagination or have been used fictitiously and are not to be construed as real. Any resemblance to persons, living or dead, actual events, locale or organizations is entirely coincidental.

All Rights Are Reserved. No part of this book may be used or reproduced in any manner whatsoever without written permission, except in the case of brief quotations embodied in critical articles and reviews.

First Samhain Publishing, Ltd. electronic publication: November 2011
First Samhain Publishing, Ltd. print publication: October 2012

Dedication

To Mom, who agreed to babysit my little angels while I took Dusty to his first Steampunk Ball. Why is it they'll follow Nana's rules without a whimper, but not Mom's? I want to know what you bribe them with! And do I get any? It's gotta be some good stuff...

To Dad, who still loves to tell embarrassing stories about me to people I don't know. You had to know I could hear you, right?

Finally, to Dusty, who looked damn good in his cowboy-steampunk outfit. I only have one thing to say: *giddy-up*!

Chapter One

Shane studied the statue, currently sitting in the window of one of New York's finest art galleries, with a critical eye. He gestured toward the assistant in the window to adjust it, stepping back again to view the results. He shook his head, still not satisfied. "The lighting's wrong."

One of the gallery's employees rushed forward and began to change the lighting shining down on the piece. He coughed, trying to hide his amusement as the gallery owner flittered around him like a manic butterfly, breath misting in the chill evening air. The pooka always seemed nervous whenever Shane dropped by. "We're so sorry, Mr. Joloun. We'll fix it right away."

"It's no problem, Mr. Klaussner. I know this was a last minute addition and I'm just happy you were able to accommodate my request."

The little man fluttered some more, pleased with himself. Bart Klaussner had been one of the first gallery owners to give him a break, and Shane had made sure he got as many showings as he could handle. Shane was loyal to those who'd helped him along the way, and if his success helped Klaussner, so much the better. "Yes, Mr. Joloun. If I may say, it's a wonderful piece. Possibly one of your finest."

Shane allowed his smile to break through. "Thank you. It's very special to me."

"It's a shame it's not for sale."

Shane shook his head, his eyes drawn once more to the magnificent flying figure he'd tried to capture in his art. "No. I'd never sell this piece."

He ignored the way the gallery owner stared at him. Instead, he enjoyed the way the light shone on the gleaming metal sculpture. It came nowhere near how wonderful she actually looked in flight. The graceful curve of her wings, the gleaming gold of her horns, the fire and passion in her every movement captivated him. The cold chrome and brass sculpture was merely an homage to the woman who'd captured him, heart and soul.

"What did you say this piece was called again, Mr. Joloun?"

Shane grinned, not surprised when the gallery owner took a step back. He had a good idea what his expression looked like. It was getting harder and harder to hide the hunger riding him for the woman who had stolen his soul. "*Akane.*"

The child of Dunne will one day perform an act that will change our world. And with those simple words from the Seer, Akane's world had been changed, possibly forever. Instead of dancing around New York, Milan, Paris, Monte Carlo and Los Angeles, she was stuck on a farm in Nebraska babysitting one of the most annoying men she'd ever met in her life. Except when her charge chose to disappear on her, that was.

"God damn it, Farm Boy. Where the hell are you? I don't have time for this shit." Akane Russo stomped through the slushy New York streets and wished she had time for a little shopping. Here she was in Manhattan, surrounded by luxury, and she couldn't do crap about it. Shane Dunne had disappeared from his Nebraska farm and the Hob wanted to know where he was—pronto. It was a pretty stupid stunt for

Shane to pull, considering the danger his family was in from the Black Court and the Malmayne clan. They'd already kidnapped him once and tortured his sister-in-law to get what they wanted. So what the hell was he thinking, running off to New York by himself? She'd thought better of him, but apparently she was wrong. When most people had the Black Court on their asses they hid behind the Blades like good little boys and girls. Shane, the idiot, just hopped a plane and headed on a merry little jaunt to New York on some kind of lunatic holiday.

The man was a moron. She no longer had any doubts about that.

She turned a corner and snarled. It was starting to snow again, the cold flakes dripping down the back of her neck, below the collar of her cashmere sweater. "Feh. I hate the cold."

She sniffed the cold air, desperate for a scent of the Nebraskan, but all she got was exhaust fumes and the frustration of every New Yorker stuck trudging through the slush with her. "I'm going to kick his ass when I find him. Kick it and then drag it back home."

She paused, then shook her head. Home? Since when had the Dunne farm become home? Akane was a city girl through and through. No Green Acres for this Prada-wearing female, thank you very much. Akane crossed the street, glaring at a cabby who dared honk his horn at her.

It was time she "looked" for Shane. She just needed to find a nice, quiet spot to do so, one where she wouldn't be disturbed for a few seconds. She found it, ducking into a doorway and staring up at the sky like she was hoping for the snow to stop falling. Which, however you looked at it, she sort of was.

Akane allowed her inner eye to open. The pale star in the center of her left iris expanded, granting her that second sight she so relied on in her work. She focused her thoughts on

Shane, picturing his striking red-gold hair, his sparkling sapphire eyes, his scarred farmer's hands that had cradled hers so gently.

A swirl of power filled her vision, that green and gold signifying his mixed blood, leprechaun and Sidhe. Beneath that swirling light was Shane, but whatever it was he was doing she couldn't tell. The light of his power blinded her to his actions.

Shit. She'd never find Jethro at this rate. She closed down her inner sight with a sigh. She was tired, her feet were cold, and she wanted a latte in the worst way, but if she didn't find Shane soon her ass was going to be a chew toy for Robin's hobgoblins.

She stepped out of the doorway and winced as the last of the evening light glinted off of something metal in the window next to her. She turned her head to catch whatever it was that had reflected the light.

Akane gasped. She was staring in the window of an art gallery. There, on a black pedestal, surrounded by black velvet, was a silver and brass sculpture. It rose majestically from some sort of crystal base, seeming to float in the air. It swirled and dipped with ballerina-like grace, dainty and feminine despite the masculine medium of metal and glass. She stepped closer to the window, enchanted, almost breathless at the sense of flight the figure exuded. She could see wings quivering in the lines of the piece as if it just waited for a moment, a breath and it would take off, forever free. It spoke of strength, elegance, and a fierce desire to fly.

She wanted it in a way she wanted very little else. The dragoness half of her blood yearned for the piece in a way not even a diehard chocoholic at the window of a Godiva store could comprehend. She glanced down at the card at the base of the statue, wondering who'd created the piece and if she could afford it. When she read the name of the piece she stopped breathing.

Akane, by Shane Joloun. Not For Sale.

Shane Joloun.

"What the hell?" She stomped into the art gallery. Dear gods, she could smell Shane all over the place, his scent rich and earthy and oh so tempting. She grabbed the first person in a suit she caught. "Excuse me, can I speak to the owner please?"

The owner was soon fetched. "My name is Mr. Klaussner. How may I help you?"

There was something odd about the man's scent. She took a deep breath, nodding to herself when she smelled pooka and something else, something elusive. He was definitely fae, that was certain.

The gallery owner eyed her designer attire and his demeanor changed from simple curiosity to an almost puppyish charm.

"The piece in the window. Who made it?"

The man smiled, all charm. He didn't even question why she didn't just read the placard under the piece. Her obvious wealth allowed her some eccentricities. "Shane Joloun, of course. He's become a famous sculptor in the last five years, and we were thrilled to have a hand in introducing him to the art world." She nodded, for once speechless. Shane was an artist?

Jethro?

Seriously?

Her eyes strayed back to the sculpture in the window.

He'd named that exquisite piece *Akane*.

The manager's voice broke into her thoughts before they

could go too far in a direction she really didn't want them to. "Would you like to see other pieces by him? We were lucky enough to get a shipment, and of course the artist himself was here until just a short while ago, helping us arrange them."

She followed behind the little man, stunned by what was on display. Shane's work was, without a doubt, the most stunning she'd ever seen. His sculptures sang, wept, took flight and left you breathless, wanting more. She couldn't take her eyes off them. Metal, glass and stone were his playthings, and he shaped them into objects that fed her soul and touched her heart. She desperately wanted to reach out, caress them. Own them, so she could look upon them whenever she desired and feel her heart was full.

She pointed to one in particular that spoke to her. It reminded her of a cat on the prowl, but there was something oddly human in the features. Something female. There was a hint of mischief in the way the cat held its tail, a playfulness despite the glittering unsheathed claws. "I want that one."

"Yes, Miss—"

"I'm not finished." She'd spotted another, one she needed for Jaden, her partner and one of Shane's new brothers-in-law. Three faceless figures writhed in glass flame and metal shadow, backs arched, hands clenched around one another, two bowed over one protectively. What struck her as oddly appropriate was that it *wasn't* the smallest figure being protected. To her, that middle figure represented Jaden, and everything he'd thought he'd lost when Duncan had Claimed Moira with a single kiss.

Where others might see only pain in the figures she saw pleasure, and battles overcome. Had Shane created it with his sister and her two bondmates in mind? "And that one." It was a perfect gift to give to the newly minted lord of Clan Blackthorn and his family. And she bet the one who would appreciate the symbolism the most would be Duncan, Jaden's bondmate and the former lord of the Malmayne clan.

"Ah. Yes." Mr. Klaussner signaled to his employee, who placed a Sold placard in front of both pieces.

She reached into her purse and held out her credit card, not surprised when the man's eyes went wide. It was an extremely rare card, given only to the very wealthy, and Mr. Klaussner's gaze ate it up before he could shield them. "You say the artist was here until just a short while ago?" When Klaussner nodded she smiled, all innocence. With her small size and big, unusual eyes, she'd gotten more than one man to do what she wanted with just a look. "Is there any chance I could meet with him?"

Klaussner shook his head sadly, the credit card cradled in his fingers. "I'm sorry, Miss—" he glanced down at the card, "—Russo, but Mr. Joloun has already returned to his family estate. I believe he went straight to the airport from here."

The family estate could mean only one thing. Shane had gone back to Nebraska. "Thank you, Mr. Klaussner." She smiled again, amused when the man's cheeks flushed.

"Where may I have the sculptures shipped to, if I may ask?"

Akane rattled off Jade's address, knowing the vampire wouldn't mind her using it, especially since one of the pieces was for him. Klaussner barely batted an eye when she said Nebraska, but his shoulders tensed just a hair. Deep inside it pleased her that this man was protective of Shane, even if it was only for the money the artist made the gallery owner.

She thanked Klaussner and stepped back out into the New York evening. Shane was on his way home, and it was time to report in to Robin. She spared one last, wistful glance at the sculpture in the window, her heart staggered once more by its beauty. Could it be that this was the way Shane saw her?

Truly?

Her hand was on the cold glass before she realized it, reaching for the beautiful artwork she couldn't take her eyes off. She snatched her hand back and stepped away, yanking her gaze from the window. She set off briskly, hailing a cab to take her back to her hotel room. She'd need to pack and appraise Robin of Shane's return to Nebraska quickly, before she found herself back in the art gallery, surrounded once more by Shane. She didn't think her heart would be able to withstand it if she stayed there even a moment longer.

If she did, it might no longer be hers.

"Sir? You saw?"

Shane stepped out of the shadows and grinned. Her reaction had been even better than he'd hoped for. "I saw. Thanks, Mr. Klaussner."

"You're quite welcome, Mr. Joloun." Klaussner waved at his assistant again, and the man, apparently psychic from what Shane could tell, answered the unspoken command. He began to carefully remove *Akane* from the window and replaced it with another one of Shane's sculptures, complete with placard and price. "Shall I have it shipped back to your studio, Mr. Joloun?"

"Please do." As if Shane would allow *Akane* to be sent to anyone's home but his own. This one was special. This one was *theirs*, and some day Akane would accept it, and the artist, and all that went with them. Until then, until the day he could Claim and Bind his mate to him, *Akane* would stay with him.

Shane grinned as the assistant wheeled *Akane* to the back of the gallery and through the storeroom doors. He couldn't wait.

He thanked the gallery owner and left. He pulled out his cell phone and dialed a number he'd long since learned by heart. "She's going home."

"Good. She saw your sculpture?"

"Yup. And she reacted the way you predicted she would."

A soft, feminine laugh sounded in his ear. "Did you make her present yet?"

Shane grinned. He'd been working on Akane's birthday present since the day he met her. "It's almost complete. I have the final component now. I'll finish it once I'm back in my studio."

"Wonderful. I look forward to hearing my daughter's screams of frustration."

I look forward to hearing your daughter scream for an entirely different reason. "I'm sure she'll find many hours of pleasure in it."

"I'm certain she will as well. Have a good flight, Shane."

"Thank you, Seer." Shane hung up and took a deep, happy breath. So far everything was going the way he'd hoped it would. He was allowing little bits and pieces of the *real* Shane to shine through for his mate, just enough to tease, to tantalize, to keep the dragoness sneaking closer and closer instead of driving her away. Akane had no desire to have a mate, but as far as he was concerned it was already too late.

She had one, and she'd learn to love him whether she wanted to or not. And if she doubted that?

Well. She'd never dealt with a determined Nebraska farm boy before. Akane was in for a rude awakening if she thought for one moment he was ever going to let her get away.

He remembered his first sight of her, her long, meticulously curled black hair gleaming in the moonlight as she tried to fake him out. She'd acted all innocent, her huge, strange eyes wide, her pouty lips pursed in a smile. Her mother's Japanese heritage was all over her. With her almond-shaped eyes and small nose she'd looked like an anime doll brought to life. It was only in her dragon form her father's ancestry shone through, from the tips of her wings to the slash of her tail. She'd turned out to be a tiny little thing when he finally got her out of her car, barely five feet tall if he were to guess, with a waist his hands could span easily and a temper that could light the world on fire. All of it was hidden behind an assumed innocence that made him laugh just to think of it. And her eyes...oh, those gorgeous eyes of hers. Shane got hard with just a glance from of those incredible eyes. One eye was a pure light hazel; the other, dark brown with a startling light hazel star in the center. Black brows were a straight slash above them, giving her a stern expression, and were probably a truer indication of the woman than the big eyes and pouty mouth.

Gods, he wanted that mouth in the worst way.

"Shane Dunne, is that you?"

Shane froze. That haughty voice was familiar. "Henri Malmayne. What a surprise." He turned to face the blond man and his equally blonde companions. Henri was the new White Court lord of the Malmayne clan, duly appointed by Glorianna herself once she'd removed Duncan Malmayne as lord. She'd removed him because his new brother-in-law had mated not just Shane's baby sister but his bond-brother, the vampire Jaden Blackthorn. Glorianna hated vampires with an unholy passion. It was unheard of for any of her people, let alone the lord of a clan as powerful as the Malmaynes to have a vampiric mate. Most vampires who chose not to walk on the dark side were Gray Court for that reason.

The problem was, the Queen of the White Court had put in place a lord whose allegiance was, at best, murky. At worst, Henri was working with the Black Court to control a prophecy he couldn't possibly understand. Shane himself was still uncertain what was supposed to happen. How could Henri hope to even begin to comprehend it? All they had to go on was the Seer's obscure words: *A child of Dunne will change the world as we know it.* Being the Malmaynes, they'd latched onto Leo, the most Sidhe of the Dunnes, thinking his seed would provide the much sought-after child. They'd kidnapped Shane first. When they hadn't been able to force Leo's compliance, they'd kidnapped Ruby, Leo's bondmate, and tortured her, all for a few vague words.

Worst of all, they'd used Black Court help to do it.

"Why would you be surprised? The Malmaynes have many businesses in New York." Cecelia Malmayne was hanging all over her cousin Henri, smirking at Shane like he was dog poo she'd narrowly avoided stepping in. "What are you doing here? Hoping to catch some culture?"

Her sister, Constance, merely looked confused, as if she couldn't understand what a rube like him was doing out of the sticks. Didn't these people know one of the richest humans in America lived in Omaha? That it was counted among the top ten cities to live and work in?

He gave the blonde bitch his biggest, goofiest smile. It seemed to drive women like her insane. "Gee, Miz Malmayne, I sure do hope so." He resisted rolling his eyes. His father might not be as politically powerful as the Malmaynes, but he was just as rich as they were. Leprechauns were good at making money, especially in land development. But because he chose to live his life working his land, Sidhe like the Malmaynes looked down on the Dunnes.

Idiots.

Something flashed before his eyes, and Shane took a quick step back and to the side. "Y'all watch out for that—"

Henri, Cecelia and Constance shrieked as a cab pulled up

to the curb in a sudden, lurching stop, spraying them with slushy, filthy water.

"Cab." Holding back his grin, Shane opened its door and climbed in. "It was sure nice seein' ya!" He grinned once more, knowing exactly how he looked: non-threatening. Their low grumbles were music to his ears as he slammed the door shut and the cab pulled away, the cabbie snickering quietly all the while.

"God, I hate them."

Shane stared at the cabbie. Huh. A sudden, clean breeze in the otherwise sealed cab told him all he needed to know. "Are they giving the sylphs here grief?"

"The sylphs, the brownies, the sprites, you name it. Anyone of the quote-unquote lesser fae have to deal with their shit. Fuckin' assholes." The sylph hit a red light and turned, his bright blue eyes full of laughter. "You're the hybrid, aintcha?"

Shane blinked. "Um..." How the fuck did this guy know who he was?

The cabbie grinned and turned back around. "You keep giving Akane a run for her money. She'll give in." He sniggered. "Eventually."

"You know her?"

"She saved my sister from a Black Court vampire. Tore the fucker's head clean off his shoulders. As far as I'm concerned, she walks on water and turns shit into gold."

"She's mentioned me?"

The cabbie laughed. "Let's just say you're gettin' under her skin."

Shane turned to look out the side window with a wicked grin. "Good."

He barely acknowledged the fae's chuckle. He had to get

home before Akane did, or the jig would be up. He'd fly into Omaha and make his way to his studio. If she arrived at the farm before he did, he could always claim truthfully that he'd been there, working on a new piece. His fingers twitched, eager to get his hands back on his work, the visions driving him into the studio almost as strong as his desire to have Akane for his own.

She'd found another piece of him now, another something he'd managed to keep hidden from her. He couldn't wait until he was with her again. Had she managed to puzzle anything else out?

And maybe, just maybe, he'd steal a kiss from his dragon and find out what fire really tasted like.

Akane pulled up outside the Dunne farmhouse. It was an old Victorian, stately and tall. It was difficult to tell the color in the dark, but it was a soothing blue, the trim a blinding white. A huge wrap-around porch with a real porch swing gave the old Victorian a homey feel.

Hell. There was that word again: home. She couldn't let herself get too attached to this place, or the people in it. She was a Blade, and one of Robin's finest assassins. She couldn't afford what a loving family would do to her.

Akane yawned so hard her jaw ached. Gods, she was weary. At least Robin had put his personal plane at her disposal, allowing her some peace on the long flight from Nebraska to New York and back again. But the drive from Omaha to the farm had forced her to acknowledge exactly how exhausted she was. She could use a good long soak in the tub and a quiet night to recharge and refresh. She'd never learned the knack of sleeping on a plane. Something about sleeping while flying just sat wrong with her.

She stepped out of her brand new Porsche Boxster and ran her fingers down the gleaming black finish. God, she loved this car. If Shane did anything to her new baby she'd rip his gonads off. It was his fault the last one had gotten blasted to smithereens. If he hadn't hidden it in the barn the day Charles Malmayne had sent the redcaps to attack the Dunne farm, the salamander would never have blown it to bits.

At the sound of a deep bark she grinned. "Sal!" She crouched down, accepting ferocious doggie kisses from the fifty-pound German shepherd. A lick of fire danced across her skin as the dog wiggled, happily welcoming its mistress home.

"Do I get a kiss too?"

Akane fell on her ass at the sound of that deep drawl. "Fuck."

"Well, I thought that might come later, but if you're that eager..."

She glared up at the man who'd managed to give her more than one sleepless night. He was grinning down at her, his big, scarred hands deep in his pockets, his butt resting on the hood of the car. He had one ankle crossed over the other.

"Get your ass off my car, Jethro."

That grin widened a hair. "Well, shucks, Miz Akane. Is this one of those ek-spen-sive cars?"

She rolled her eyes and took the hand he offered her. She found herself standing way too close for comfort. "It's worth more than your hospital stay will be if you don't move."

He chuckled, the big bastard, and rolled easily up and off the car, his arms wrapping around her. She reared back as much as she could as his big head lowered, but despite her dragon heritage she couldn't quite bend back far enough. Shane took her mouth in a careful, questing kiss, as if he understood she could and would bite him if he pushed too far.

Part of her hoped he would do just that. Shane tasted incredible, with just an undertone of something rich and metallic. Her inner dragon purred, but Akane held the sound back. No way could she let him know how much she enjoyed the intimate touch.

He released her and took a step back, staring at her with wistful greed. The wistfulness was gone almost as quickly as it appeared, but the fact it had been there, that he wanted her that badly, sent her heart racing. "Welcome home, Akane."

She hid her shiver as best she could, but damn it. His voice did things to her, especially when he used that deep, warm tone he only directed at her. "This isn't home." She sniffed and almost stomped past him, remembering at the last minute the dirt driveway beneath her three inch heels.

"More home than you've ever had before."

She paused; something about his tone set her back up. "I don't know what you're talking about."

His rich laugh followed her into the brightly lit house. The cream-colored walls and dark, sturdy wooden furniture wasn't her taste, but Aileen and Sean Dunne fit right in here. They'd blended early American with a number of pieces they'd moved from Ireland for a look uniquely their own. Framed prints of Ireland mingled with family portraits. The dark green fabrics of the furniture grounded the softer, cheerful yellows Aileen had strewn about the room in the form of pillows and flowers. The only odd note was an amethyst vase Leo Dunne had given his mother, sitting in pride of place on the mantelpiece. Akane took a deep breath and felt something tight within her ease at the now familiar scents of raw earth, polished wood and family.

She blinked.

Family? Since fucking when?

She growled low in her throat and headed for the kitchen,

knowing Aileen Joloun Dunne wouldn't be happy if Akane didn't stop in to say hello before heading to her room. She shrugged off the thought of *her room*, plastering a smile on her face for Aileen's sake.

"Gods, child, you look exhausted. Here, have a seat and I'll make you a nice cup of tea." Aileen's soft Irish accent had a bit of Brit in it, marking her as from one of Ireland's conquering families. The fact that Aileen Dunne considered herself Irish through and through would have had no effect on those intent on destroying anything British back when the IRA flourished. It was probably why Sean Dunne had moved his family to America in the first place.

"You're a saint, Aileen." She glared as Shane made his way into the room, gifting his mother with a kiss on the cheek. "Unlike some people I know."

Aileen's tinkling laugh filled the room. "Ah, now. Have you two been fighting again?" Her hair fell to her waist, a straight, shining curtain of glowing red-gold just a touch darker than her son's. Slightly tilted green eyes the color of emeralds peeked out from under the longest, most lush lashes Akane had ever seen. Her chin was delicately pointed, her nose fine and aristocratic, her lips full and pink. She could see the resemblance between Moira, Aileen's daughter and Jaden's female bondmate, and her mother, but she could find little of the woman in either of Aileen's tall sons.

"A wonderful sound to come home to." Sean Dunne stepped in from the cold, his wool-lined jacket a shade of green exactly matching his wife's eyes. He stepped in for his own kiss from Aileen, but where Shane's had been filial Sean's was that of a man marking his territory.

Now here was where she saw Shane. Oh, Shane mostly had his mother's coloring, but when it came to size and shape, he was his father's son. Tall and strong, Sean Dunne was head and shoulders above his dainty wife, with gleaming dark hair and eyes the color of a summer sky. Shane had his father's eyes, but deeper, more intense, as if something in Sean had been refined within his oldest son.

She turned to find Shane studying her, watching her reaction to his father's kiss. She raised her brows and leaned back in her chair, daring him to comment.

When he did nothing more than give her that knowing, irritating grin she turned back to his parents. "How are Ruby and Leo?"

Aileen's shoulders tensed for a brief moment. "They're fine. Settled in nicely. Leo's business is on hold until this Child of Dunne shite is taken care of."

Akane almost gasped. Aileen hadn't cursed the entire month she'd known the woman, at least not in polite company. It wasn't the way the Sidhe lady had been raised.

She caught sight of Sean's worried look. Aileen had to be more upset than Akane had thought. "I will fix this. I give you my word." She meant it too. Shane aside, the Dunne family had been good to her.

Aileen smiled at her. "I know you're doing your best, Akane, and we're grateful for it." A mug of tea was placed in front of her, sweetened just the way she liked it. "And I think you'll be wanting a bath after this?"

Akane nodded. She was so tired she couldn't see straight, but damn if she'd let Jethro see that. "Yeah. A bath sounds nice."

That annoying grin was off Shane's face. "Bedtime right after." The command in his voice matched the challenge in his expression. He practically dared her to disobey him.

If Akane wasn't so tired she'd take him up on that dare.

"Shane." The warning in his father's voice would have amused her if she wasn't so drained.

"Da, I know what I'm doing."

The two men exchanged an enigmatic look, but to her surprise, Sean backed down first. "All right, then." He brushed a brief, surprising kiss across the top of Akane's head. "I'll go change, then. We'll keep the house quiet tonight, Akane. Get some rest." And he sauntered out of the room, Aileen's eyes glued to her mate's back.

The speculation in them was soon turned on Shane, who held up his hands, his expression all innocence. "What?"

Aileen's gaze narrowed. "Hmph."

When Shane merely chuckled, she shook her head and turned back to the stove.

The dinner simmering on top would normally have tempted Akane to steal at least a bite, but she was at the point of tired where she was feeling nauseated. She stood and went to the sink, rinsed out her cup and placed it carefully in the dishwasher. "I'm going to call it a night."

Aileen's hand reached out and cupped her chin. The Sidhe was taller than she was, but not by much. Then again, most adults were taller than Akane. "Sleep, child. We'll let Sal keep watch again."

She smiled. Sal, the salamander she'd defeated when it had been ordered to attack the Dunne farm, had bonded to her. It was as loyal as any guard dog, as playful as a puppy and adored the Dunnes. It had been the right decision to leave him here to protect them in her absence. "Good night, Aileen." She glared at Shane, who was stuffing a chocolate chip cookie in his big mouth. "Jethro."

He waved merrily at her. "Night, Miz Akane." He grinned, goo from the cookie stuck to his teeth.

"Ugh." She shuddered and walked out of the kitchen, the sound of Shane's laugh a balm to her soul, unwanted though it was.

"Are you ever going to stop teasing that girl?"

Shane picked up the tea his mother set in front of him. He swished some around in his mouth before answering his mother. "Stop? Why? She enjoys herself way too much for me to stop."

His mother bopped him on the back of the head with the flat of her hand. "Shane Joloun, do not make me break out the wooden spoon."

He laughed up at his mother, adoring the way her face lit up. "Trust me. I've got inside information."

"Oh?" Aileen pulled up a chair and propped her chin in her hand.

"Subtle, Ma." He took another sip of his tea, smiling when the water in the upstairs bath started. Akane would soon be naked and wet. Too bad he couldn't do anything about that yet.

"I try."

"Let's put it this way." He leaned in and whispered in his mother's ear. "I have her mom on speed dial."

Aileen's head dropped onto the table. "She's going to kill you when she finds out."

He leaned back and propped his feet on the chair across from him. "Then I can't let her find out, can I?" He grinned at his mother. "Besides, you'll protect me."

Aileen's hand reached out. She smacked him on the back of the head again, all without lifting her own head from the table. "You'd better hope she understands, Shane. She's the type who will walk away from you if she thinks you've been playing with her."

He set his cup back on the table. "Then it's a good thing I'm not playing." He stood and pressed a kiss to his mother's head. "I'm heading into the studio for a bit. I have something I need to do."

She lifted her head. "Shall I have your father bring you dinner?"

"Please." He paused, one hand on the doorknob, the other holding his coat. "Thanks, Ma."

She smiled at him. "You're welcome."

Shane headed out into the cold evening, the visions swirling in his head beating a tattoo behind his eyes. His hands twitched, eager to get hold of his tools. He had a piece to make, maybe two, and it would take some time to get everything right.

But first, he was going to finish his mate's birthday present. He had just the thing to set in the center, something that would make his lovely dragon gasp with pleasure. He just hoped she appreciated the effort he'd put into acquiring it.

Shane walked behind the house for about fifteen minutes to where his father had helped him build his studio. They'd paid quite a bit to have electricity run to the out-of-the-way area, but it had been worth it. Shane was able to use every tool he needed to create his "art", and in return his father had learned there was more to Shane's work than either of them had expected.

Shane opened the thick door and pulled it closed behind him. He flicked on the light switch, grateful he'd heated the place twenty-four-seven. Already he could feel his toes thawing. He hung his coat on the hook next to the front door and toed off his sneakers. He pulled open the door leading to the changing room where he kept the coveralls he wore when he worked. The changing room had a washer and dryer as well as storage for his shoes and clothes. He grabbed a fresh set of coveralls, changed quickly and slipped on the steel-toed boots he only wore in the studio. The amount of glass dust and metal filings embedded in the leather made them impractical to wear anywhere else.

Shane exited the changing room and made his way into the main part of the studio. A few finished pieces graced pedestals around the room, but most of the pedestals were empty. He'd shipped most of the finished works to Klaussner, but there were a couple he refused to part with.

And soon *Akane* would be back here.

Shane ran his fingers down the one piece he considered giving away. The entwined lovers were done in solid silver, but the collar around the woman's throat was set with fiery ruby chips, while an onyx ring decorated the hand of the male figure. It had taken him quite a while to get the figures correct. For a short time the shadow of a third had tried to taint the purity of the piece, but in the end Shane had known what he had to do.

He'd allowed himself to be kidnapped, and in doing so had set things in motion that were still rocking his family's world.

Shane picked up the piece and took it to the back room. He was going to ship this to his big brother. Leo and Ruby would adore it.

He chuckled quietly. Akane was in for a shock when she got her credit card statement. Oh, the cougar he'd done and she'd purchased would show up, but the sculpture of Jaden, Moira and Duncan would arrive at the Blackthorn home without a dime being paid for it. He'd always intended to give that piece to Moira, but it had wound up in the shipping box by accident. He still didn't know what he'd been thinking when he'd packed it with the others, but Akane's reaction had made the mistake worth it.

And maybe it hadn't been a mistake. Maybe Akane had

been meant to see that piece. Shane didn't know for sure, and he doubted he ever would. Some things, despite his powers, remained a mystery to him.

Shane carefully set down the silver figures and headed toward the room where he worked his real magic. It would take some time to gather the materials he'd need to make the new sculptures. For the first piece he'd need sea glass and silver; for the second...well. He took a look around the studio and picked up one of the jagged pieces of metal left over from another project. He'd summon what he needed for the figure, but for the rest? He already had what he needed.

Shane took a seat on the hard metal stool he tended to move around his workspace. He placed his hands on the empty wooden table in front of him and closed his eyes, visualizing what he needed, knowing he'd get almost what he wanted. The silver would be raw, unrefined. The sea glass would need to be shaped. But he'd have the raw materials to begin his new project. He concentrated, his magic surging through him, the feel of something just beyond his reach becoming stronger. He strained, grasping for the edges of the silver with his mind, finally grabbing hold and pulling it to him with a gasp.

Shane opened his eyes. On the table sat a huge lump of raw silver. Sweat dripped into his eyes and he reached up, wiping it away before it could begin to sting.

"That never fails to amaze me."

Shane jumped. "Fucking hell, Da!"

His father's rich laugh rolled through the studio. "Sorry, Shane." His father placed a steaming bowl of soup and hot biscuits on the table next to the lump of silver ore. "Dinner."

"Thanks." Shane picked up the soup bowl and began eating, shoveling the soup in like it was his first meal in days. Creating raw materials took a great deal of energy. By the time he was through creating everything he needed, he'd collapse onto the small bed in his tiny bedroom, exhausted.

"It still amazes me to see you do that." Sean poked the ore, his expression bemused. "One of these days you'll have to explain how you do it."

"Simple." Shane grabbed one of the biscuits. It was still piping hot. How his father managed that neat little trick in this cold he'd never figured out. To him, that was real magic. "I make dreams reality."

His father nodded. "I know."

Shane grinned and shoveled in the food, a peaceful silence dropping between the two men.

Akane woke the next day more refreshed than she'd felt in quite some time. The bed was soft, the birds were chirping, and the strong arm around her waist was comforting. She snuggled in deeper and found herself cradled against a strong chest. "Mmm."

Her only answer was a light snore.

Akane stifled her giggle. Jethro snored? It was so...adorable.

Akane blinked. *Wait a minute.* She turned her head, hoping that somehow she was still dreaming.

Nope. There was a huge lump of Nebraskan in her bed, snoring and drooling on her pillow. "Shane."

He snuffled and pulled her tighter to him. One thick thigh covered both her legs.

"Jethro." She tugged on his chest hairs, hoping the pain would wake him up.

"Akane."

No one, most especially Shane, had the right to moan her

name like that. "Wake up, Shane."

One huge paw slid up her hip. His face nuzzled into her neck, his whiskers abrasive. Tantalizing. She could almost feel that beard brushing the skin of her inner thighs.

Gah. Mind out of the gutter! If this continued she'd probably find her ankles somewhere around his ears followed shortly by an Awkward Morning After Moment. So in sheer self defense she grabbed hold of his nipple and twisted it. "WAKE! UP!"

She didn't know that the Dunnes had Banshee blood in them. When her ears stopped ringing she found herself pinned to the bed by one angry half-Sidhe, half-leprechaun hybrid. His sapphire eyes had darkened to near black, his reddish blonde hair stuck up in messy spikes and whorls around his head. His lips were pressed firmly together.

So were her legs.

"Was that really necessary?" Shane's deep, easy-going drawl was thickened by sleep and annoyance.

He'd managed to get hold of her wrists and pin her hands beside her head, something she didn't realize until she tried to push him off. "Yes."

"You think waking a man with a purple nurple is appropriate?"

"In certain circumstances, yes."

A truly evil grin took over his face. "Then I'm certain you'll understand why I find this equally appropriate."

Akane's eyes went wide as Shane swooped down, taking her mouth in a kiss that threatened to unlock her legs. Before she could stop herself her lips parted, letting him in. Shane took immediate advantage, thrusting his tongue into her mouth with an intensity that told her how he'd thrust his cock into her body. He'd take her, leaving her no doubt as to who she was with, who she belonged to.

His flavor burst over her, feral, deep and strong. It was a taste she could easily find herself addicted to. His hands curled around hers as somehow he took the kiss deeper. She found herself breathing him in, his scent surrounding her, his taste filling her. His hard cock nudged her stomach. For a brief moment of insanity she allowed her thighs to relax.

For some reason, Shane didn't take advantage of the implied invitation. Instead the kiss softened, became something more than just need, stronger than just hunger. Something tingled and danced across her skin, like snow fairies, cold and delicate. Akane risked opening her eyes.

Gold and green sparks lit the air around them. The son of a bitch's Sidhe half was trying to Claim her.

Before she could buck him off he ended the kiss. "Damn, girl." He groaned, his forehead resting against hers, his hips rocking into her, dragging his cock along the silk of her pajama pants. "Just...damn."

"Get off me."

He blinked, looking shocked at the harsh, growled words. "Akane."

"I am *not* your gods-damned mate, Shane."

His head tilted. For one brief moment she thought it was anger coloring his features before it was completely swamped by determination. "Fight it all you want. Yell. Scream. Throw things." He blinked, his lips twitching. "But not in my mother's living room." He almost succeeded in winning a smile from her. His lips brushed the tip of her nose. "But we both know you're mine."

She growled up at him. In about five seconds smoke would literally pour out of her ears if he didn't get off her. "You're delusional."

He smiled, an expression so full of joy she was shocked. "No. I'm blessed." He brushed another soft kiss across her nose before slowly climbing out of bed. She tried to ignore the way his pajama pants rode low on his hips, or the way his hard cock tented the flannel fabric. He stretched, his arms over his head, his hands almost touching the ceiling. The long line of his back arched, his muscles bunched, and Akane had to stifle a groan of her own. He finished stretching and shook himself. "Coffee." She watched in disbelief as he sauntered toward the bedroom door. "C'mon, darlin' time's awastin'." He sent her a heart-stopping grin and opened the door. "My woman has bad guy ass to kick, remember?"

Her jaw dropped. He winked and, without another glance, left the bedroom, shutting the door quietly behind him.

Akane picked up the pillow he'd been drooling on and, with an ear-splitting shriek, threw it at the door. She could not allow herself to be drawn in by Jethro. She was a fucking *Blade*! A total badass! Men quivered in fear when she appeared irritated. Fae hid in whatever nooks and crannies they could force themselves into at the sound of her wings. She ate Black Court vampires for breakfast and thought nothing of having lunch with the Hob afterward. She had Louis Vuitton on speed dial and could buy the Dunne farm a thousand times over.

And Shane thought the whole thing was what? Cool? Neat? Fucking *cute?*

Akane's jaw clenched. If Shane thought a few sparkly lights were going to make *this* dragoness settle down on the farm, he had another thing coming.

Akane blinked. The drifting scent of freshly brewed coffee filled her senses. Her mouth watered at the thought of one of Aileen's perfect breakfasts. Was she making pancakes? Akane *loved* pancakes. *Then again, maybe I could stay here for a while.*

"Aren't you out of bed yet?" Shane's laughing voice carried through the door. She could hear his big feet stamping down the stairs. She'd have to hustle to get anything to eat. The man ate enough food to feed three people.

Akane leapt out of bed and headed for the shower.

Chapter Two

Akane allowed the rhythm of the music to flow through her. She kept her movements sensual, tempting the man across from her in the way only a dragoness could. From the amount of drool on his chin her target was buying into it. Akane allowed some of her inner fire to seep into her expression, smiling slightly when the target almost dropped his drink in his lap.

If Robin's facts were correct, this man would lead her to information the Malmaynes would kill to keep quiet. She ran her hands through her hair, fluffing the curls around her face with a coquettish look. She licked her lips and allowed her gaze to roam over her target. When she was sure she'd set him to a nice simmer, she crooked her finger at him. All she had to do was seduce him enough that he was distracted. Her temporary Sidhe partner would then read the target's mind and extract the information they needed. But if the target sensed for even one moment that his mind had been invaded, the entire operation would have to be scrapped and the back-up plan put into action.

Akane did not want to go to plan B. Plan B involved Robin's direct involvement, something she was striving to avoid at all costs. If Robin showed up, things would get...messy.

Akane allowed the target to slide his hands around her waist. The Malmayne looked like most of them did, with golden, gleaming hair and pale eyes. On any other occasion she might have found him semi-attractive. Tonight, he was nothing more than a mark.

She danced with...what was his name again? Tristan? She danced with Tristan Malmayne, wondering when her temporary partner would give her the signal that they'd gotten what they needed. It would be a simple matter to slip away at that point, something she'd perfected over the years. More than one man had been left in her dust after she'd gotten what she wanted.

The target wasn't a bad dancer. If he hadn't been on the devil's side she might have even enjoyed herself. She ran her fingers through the hair at the nape of his neck, scraping the skin with her nails. A shiver ran through him. His pupils dilated. His erection brushed against her as he pulled her closer.

She turned in his arms, allowing him to move against her ass, hoping her partner was done. His hands roamed over her bare legs, trying to slip beneath the hem of her miniskirt. If his fingers moved two inches higher he'd find a four inch stiletto pinning his foot to the floor. She wanted gone from here before she found herself thrown over Tristan's shoulder and carted out of the bar. She'd hate to have to explain to Robin that she'd been forced to break the target into tiny little pieces for being too grabby. Again.

Akane looked up, trying to locate her partner, and damn near shrieked in surprise.

Right in front of her was one of the handsomest men she'd ever had the misfortune to meet. His sapphire eyes were blazing with anger. Dark blue silk stretched across massive shoulders. Tight, dark jeans were molded to his legs like a second skin. Those scarred hands took hold of the Tristan's and twisted, sending the Sidhe reeling back in shock and pain.

"Mine."

"Sorry." She turned to find Tristan's eyes narrowed. He studied Shane, way too closely for Akane's comfort. "Don't I know you?"

Shane grinned. "Nope." He took hold of Akane's arm and pulled her to the middle of the dance floor. "You are in deep shit, Miz Akane."

It took everything in her to keep from twisting his fat head off his neck like a bottle cap. "I'm *working*."

"That's one word for it."

She gasped in outrage. If he said that again he was going to be known as the Cockless Wonder. She allowed herself to be pulled into his arms just so she could hiss in his ear. "Do you know what you have done?"

"Nope. Don't care either."

The anger still appeared to be riding him hard. She was surprised his magic hadn't escaped his control, filling the air around them with sparks or painting the whorls of a leprechaun on his skin. Only Shane's eyes glittered with an almost inhuman rage. His attention wasn't focused on her, though. His eyes were tracking Tristan Malmayne as the man made his way back to his seat.

"Robin will be here shortly."

That got his attention. "Shit. You meant you were *working*, didn't you?"

She gritted her teeth. "How attached are you to your balls?"

He had the audacity to laugh down at her. "Pretty damn attached."

She pulled his head closer. "That was Tristan Malmayne. He might have given me an in with the Malmaynes if you hadn't fucked it up."

"They know who you are and who you work for, remember? Didn't you damn near hand out business cards the day Duncan explained to his ex-clanmates why Charles Malmayne had been executed, and by whom?"

She grimaced. True, she'd told the Malmaynes in the room who she was and backed up Duncan's declaration that Charles's execution had been legal and fully justified. That didn't mean she still couldn't work the case the way Robin had asked her to. Besides, Tristan hadn't been in that room, may not have gotten a good enough look at her through the satellite feed Duncan had set up. She could have pulled it off, especially the way Tristan's hands had been inching up her skirt.

Shane lifted his head and pulled her so close she could practically feel his heartbeat. "Your mom called. She said hi."

Akane bit him through his shirt. The son of a bitch had been talking to her mother?

He pulled her head closer with a happy sigh. "She also said happy birthday."

Akane attempted to lift her head. It was like trying to lift a Chevy Tahoe with her pinky. Damn, the man was strong. She usually snapped people like twigs when they annoyed her, but Shane was made of sterner stuff. He was the only person she'd ever met, other than Robin Goodfellow, who could physically haul her places she didn't want to go. She'd kicked him once, and instead of the satisfying sound of bones breaking, he'd barely grunted. "You're dead. You know that, right?"

She felt the rumble of his chuckle under her cheek. "Dance with me, sweetheart."

She rolled her eyes. He was not going to wiggle out of his imminent demise that easily. "Sweetheart? Since when?"

"Since the moment I saw you." He allowed her to lift her head, and she was under no illusions about that. He *allowed* it.

"No matter your form, no matter what Robin asks of you, remember one thing: you belong to me."

The song changed, slowed, and Shane began to dance. He moved against her with a sinuous grace that shocked her. For a brief, shining moment she pictured them moving together like this in bed, and she damn near came on the spot.

She had to get away from him before she did something she'd really regret, like rip those clothes off him and screw him right in the middle of the dance floor. Hell, with the way her luck was going recently Tristan Malmayne would offer to join in.

"Dance with me. Let's give Mr. Malmayne a *real* show."

Akane glared up at Shane but couldn't hold it. He was right. If she couldn't seduce Tristan the way she'd originally planned, she'd seduce him by being in someone else's arms. She followed Shane's lead, dancing with him the way she'd meant to dance with Tristan. She kept the majority of her attention on Tristan, watching him, gauging his reactions to see if it was working.

It wasn't. He'd already found himself someone new to play with, a pretty little blonde with deep brown eyes with just a hint of... "Oh shit."

"What?"

"The blonde with Tristan?"

"Yeah?"

"I'm pretty sure that's Robin."

Shane paled. Good. The man had some sense of self preservation. "Wow. He moves fast."

She exchanged glances with her partner, relieved when the man nodded and headed for the door. "Time to go."

"You have what you need?"

She looked back, only to find Tristan watching her leave

with Shane. His expression was chagrined as he realized he wouldn't get another shot at her. Little did he know. Akane planned on giving him as many shots as he wanted to take. "Yup."

She headed for the door of the bar, Shane one step behind her. When they exited the building she braced herself for an unwanted meeting with the Hob. "Etienne, did we get what we needed?"

"In a way, *oui*." The French Sidhe shrugged. "His thoughts were filled with you, but his mind is sharp. He almost detected my meddling. I was barely able to touch on the information we needed. We'll need to set something up again where he's distracted by you." Etienne gestured to the side of the building, away from a group of people heading into the bar. "Personally, I was surprised to find a Malmayne in a place like this. It's not up to their usual standards."

Akane nodded. "The lord of the manor slumming it." The place wasn't bad at all. Akane had spent many a pleasurable hour in bars much like this one, where the drinks flowed freely and the music was loud and driving. It soothed some of the wildness in her to get out on a dance floor and give in to her dragon, if only a little.

"Maybe he feels free to do so knowing Henri and the girls are in New York."

Akane and Etienne stared at Shane. "How do you know that?"

"I ran into them there briefly. I didn't stick around to chat, though. They were kind of irritated with me." Shane shrugged. "It might have been the face full of slush that did it."

Akane opened her mouth to ask, then closed it again. She did *not* want to know. She turned back to Etienne, ignoring Shane's amusement. She'd have to find out from Robin if any

Blades in New York were keeping an eye on the trio. "What did you learn?"

"Not much. He is perturbed by Henri's insistence on obtaining Leo Dunne's seed. He believes he overheard something that may mean Henri is planning another move on Ruby Dunne. But that was all I got before he began to suspect something was wrong."

"Shit." Shane moved to Akane's side, firmly putting himself in the situation. She wanted to tell him to back the fuck off, but Ruby was special. All the Dunnes adored the human Leo had mated, and with good reason. She took everything the fae had thrown at her in stride, never losing herself in what had to seem a strange, crazy world to the mundane female. She'd even managed to make Robin a good friend, a rare deed. If Robin found out Ruby was in danger once more, he'd pull out all the stops and never even tell her about it.

There would be bloodshed in the Black Court, starting with Henri Malmayne. And Robin would be far from subtle about it.

"Have they *officially* become Black Court? I thought they were still White, if only technically."

She was surprised Shane was the one who asked. She'd assumed the Malmaynes had gone Black, but if their allegiance was underground it might explain why the few good Malmaynes had remained with their clan. There were probably a few who did not approve of Henri's plans for the clan, but she bet there'd be more who would if they knew about them.

"No. Glorianna has issued no proclamations to that effect. She's still investigating the allegations on her own, and she's let stand her pronouncement of Henri as their lord." Etienne rubbed his hand through his long, dark hair. "Which means we could trip over her agents at any moment."

"Or worse, find ourselves fighting them."

"We don't know who they are or what angle they're taking. This could be bad."

"My darlings, leave Glorianna to me."

Akane jumped. She should have caught that wild, intense scent before the man spoke, but Robin had a way of creeping up on even the most sensitive noses. She turned to face her boss, her expression deliberately bland. "Good evening, Robin."

Robin Goodfellow, aka Puck, aka the Hob, one of the scariest men on the planet, was a tall, slender man with the wiry build and broad shoulders of a swimmer. He had waist-length, red hair that danced around him in a fiery halo, and laughing blue eyes in a face that would have made Michelangelo weep. The Hob was dressed tonight in a caramel-colored silk shirt that complemented his bright hair and tight leather pants that showcased his slim build. Leather boots completed the look. He looked like a fairy-tale prince with a modern twist, and he reveled in it. The Hob smiled at her, green fire flashing in his eyes.

"Good evening, Akane. Shane."

Shane smiled back, totally at ease with Robin's presence. "Hey, Robin. I'm sorry about that. I didn't know she was working. Blame me for any screw-ups back there. If she'd told me, I wouldn't have interfered."

Robin looked up at Shane through his lashes. "Truly? You could have stood by and watched as your—"

"I. Am. Not. His. Mate." Akane poked Jethro in the chest with each hissed word. She was getting tired of repeating herself.

"Whatever you say, darlin'," Shane drawled back. He caught hold of her hand and held it there against his chest. "You're just my sweetie, right?" And he gave her the biggest, most gooberish grin she'd ever seen on a person's face.

43

Gods, he was so good at looking stupid it was frightening, especially since he was one of the cagiest men she'd ever met. She looked over at Robin, desperately trying to hide the panic growing inside her. "Can I kill him now?"

Robin threw his head back and laughed.

Shane just shook his head, his grin lightening to something much more natural. "Robin, if there's anything I can do to help, let me know."

She didn't like the speculation in Robin's eyes. She didn't like it one little bit. She spoke without thinking, protecting him. "He's not Blade material."

That green fire flashed in Robin's eyes once more. "I believe I am the best judge of that."

The gentle rebuke was made more chilling by the green light that refused to leave Robin's face. Akane bowed low, baring her neck, eyes respectfully downcast. "My apologies, my lord."

She waited, head bowed, for either the blow or the caress. She breathed a sigh of relief when Robin's hand tangled in her curls. "Forgiven, of course. One must make allowances when mates are involved."

She lifted her head once more. "You're so certain of that?" She was careful to keep any challenge from her voice. Robin's temperament could be volatile; she didn't want to test the levels of his affection for her.

He tilted her face up with one black-nailed finger. "Of course." He winked at her, the green fire gone, once more the laughing rogue rather than Oberon's personal Blade. "Am I ever wrong?"

She bit her tongue until it bled.

Robin nodded as if she'd agreed with him whole-heartedly.

"Very well then. Shane, I'll keep your offer in mind. For now, we know that Tristan is less than pleased with his Malmayne cousins."

Shane's fists clenched. "And Henri is thinking of harming Ruby."

Every light bulb in the parking lot burst, plunging them into darkness. Robin's voice floated out of the darkness, mildly curious. "I'm sorry. What was that again?"

The only light now was from passing cars, and Akane was grateful for it. She didn't want to see Robin's face just then. The last time he'd used that particular tone of voice they hadn't even been able to identify the body via DNA. The Hob had managed to tear even that apart in his rage. She inched closer to Shane, placing herself between him and Robin, knowing even as she did so it would do no good.

Apparently Robin was *very* fond of the human female.

Etienne spoke after an audible gulp. "Tristan overheard something that leads him to believe Henri's planning on making a move on Ruby Dunne, something that would force Leo's hand and give them what they want."

"Ah." The soft sigh Robin gave sounded sweet and gentle. "Then Ruby, above all, must be protected. Akane, you and Etienne will continue to court Tristan. Shane, I may require your assistance, but for now, allow Akane to protect you." When Shane made a sound of protest Robin's eyes glowed, bright enough to see, eerie enough to raise goose bumps on her arms. "Shane, you are still a child of Dunne and therefore in possible danger. Allow my Blade to do her job, if you please."

Shane bowed beside her. "As you wish."

Robin's hand reached out and patted Shane's cheek. "Good. You all know what you must do." A gust of wind kicked up, swirling around Robin in a mini tornado, and yet his voice was as clear as ever. "And so do I." With that, the Hob disappeared. The wind died down. The only sounds in the parking lot now were the breathing of the three remaining fae.

Akane's damn knees had gone weak. If Robin had lost it, Shane could have died. Her reaction to that thought was something she was going to have to think long and hard about. The knowledge that she'd been willing to place herself between Shane and Robin-fucking-Goodfellow was life altering. "That went well."

Etienne touched her shoulder. "Indeed. We still breathe."

Shane blew out a breath, possibly just to prove he could. Robin had that effect on people. "He does know how to make an exit, doesn't he?"

She refused to join Etienne in his slightly hysterical giggles. A woman had her pride, after all.

When they got back to the farm, cars were parked out front. Shane grinned. His mother had managed to pull it off, and Shane couldn't be more pleased. It was one more step in giving Akane the family she so desperately craved, even if she didn't understand why.

It was enough that he did. He had no problems sharing his family with his future mate. Hell, he wanted her to claim them as her own, because they'd already begun to claim her.

"What's going on?"

He opened the car door and helped her out, hiding his smile as her covetous glance ran over Bumblebee. The bright yellow Corvette had caught her eye immediately. The low growl in her throat when she realized it belonged to him had been priceless. Since she'd flown to the bar rather than trust her Boxster in the parking lot, he'd been more than happy to give her a ride home, and she'd loved every minute of it. He'd opened up the muscle car on the road, letting the roar of the engine and the sounds of the wind drown out the need for conversation. "Let's find out."

He led her up to the front porch, noting her frown when she recognized Duncan's M6 and Leo's brand new Land Rover. "Wonder what they're doing here? You think Robin contacted them?"

He almost laughed, keeping a straight face with difficulty. "You mean about Henri and his probable villainous intent to harm Ruby?"

She glared at him. She did that a lot, but this time was different. She was eyeing him like she didn't quite know what to make of him and it was freaking her the fuck out.

"Yeah."

"Maybe." He opened the front door, enjoying her gasp of surprise. "Then again, maybe not."

Over the green sofa in the living room, his mother had strung a Happy Birthday banner. Food, drink and presents littered every available surface. Family filled the air with chatter and laughter, warming the happy home even further.

"Akane! Happy birthday." Ruby, Leo's bubbly mate, darted out from the shelter of her man's arms and gave Akane a hug.

Akane, red-faced, startled and wisps of smoke curling out her nostrils, hugged Ruby back. "Thank you."

"Let them in from the cold, child." Aileen gently rebuked Ruby, who blushed and pulled away from Akane.

"Sorry. Here, let me get your coats." Ruby shut the door and gathered their coats while Moira gave Akane a hug. Jaden and Duncan watched their female through warm, loving eyes, their own hands clasped together, dark skin twined with fair.

Jaden Blackthorn's Native American heritage was evident

in his long, black hair and eyes, the shape of his jaw and his dusky skin. Duncan Malmayne-Blackthorn was as fair as his male mate was dark, with golden blond hair and pale gray eyes. Shane's red-haired sister was like a flame between them, dancing back and forth with a touch here, a caress there, keeping her men grounded. It warmed Shane's heart to see how close they'd become. She'd nearly lost both of them, one to mate sickness and the other to self doubt, and still hadn't quite gotten over that. None of them had realized how deep the bond between Duncan and Jaden was until Jaden had left for weeks, nearly destroying both Duncan and Moira in the process. If Jaden had understood what his absence would do to his lovers he never would have left them, but he had, and Duncan still bore the marks in the silver that now dotted the golden mop of hair Jaden was busy playing with. He laughed when Duncan pushed his hands away with an annoyed grunt, but Shane caught the amusement Duncan tried to hide.

"Happy birthday, Akane." Jaden gave Akane a hug of his own, lifting the dragoness off her feet and twirling her around, much to Moira's obvious disgust.

Shane wasn't worried about Jaden. He was Akane's usual partner, working with her on the cases Robin assigned them, but he'd been so busy setting up his newly minted clan he hadn't been able to assist her recently. His presence in Nebraska must mean that his business in Colorado had been happily concluded. Shane could only hope so. He trusted Jaden to guard Akane's back much more than that Etienne guy. The Sidhe might have been dumpster diving in Tristan Malmayne's head but his beady eyes had been glued to Akane's thighs.

Seriously. What the fuck kind of name was *Etienne*?

"Thanks, Jade." Akane gave Jaden a peck on the cheek, and that *did* bother Shane. She'd yet to kiss *him* voluntarily.

Artistic Vision

The rest of the family offered their birthday wishes, and soon they were digging into the mountain of food Aileen had made. Shane found himself tucked in the corner, a plate in one hand and a glass of wine in the other, watching indulgently as his father tried to get Akane to eat asparagus tips. It was like watching him trying to feed Moira Brussel sprouts when she'd been four. Akane was making that same stinky doo-doo face Moira had made way back then.

"She seems happy enough."

Shane was very proud of the fact that he didn't jump at the sound of that rich, laughing voice. "I hope so, since I plan on her living here for the rest of her natural life." He turned to smile at the red-headed man leaning in the window. An amazing feat, since the window had been closed not a moment before, Shane hadn't heard it open, and for some reason the cold winter air wasn't coming into the house. But that was what you got when the Hob decided to drop in for supper.

The Hob stepped in through the open window, closing it silently behind him. "Is that so?" His head tilted, the gesture somehow inhuman, almost birdlike. "What does she think of that?"

Shane shrugged. "She's mine, and I'm here." He held out his plate, the sandwich on it untouched. "Food?"

Robin took the plate with a small bow. "Thank you."

While Robin ate his ham and cheese sandwich Shane took a moment to study him. Something about Robin had his fingers twitching. Just out of reach was the vision he'd had earlier, one that became stronger each time he met the Hob. With a gasp he realized what was meant to be in the center of the storm his vision kept showing him, and the knowledge left him dazed.

"Are you all right?"

Shane nodded, too stunned to speak. He needed to get to

his workspace. He needed to go *now*. The vision was riding him hard, demanding completion before it would leave him be. "Yeah." He handed his drink to Robin. "I have to go." He signaled his mother and she nodded. She understood what the look on his face meant, and where he'd be for the foreseeable future. She'd let everyone know if they asked. His family would take care of him until it was over.

"Shane."

He blinked and stared at Robin, his vision superimposed over the slender figure of the man himself. "Yes?"

Robin studied him, his brows slowly rising. "Take care. It's cold out."

"Cold out." His eyes darted longingly toward the door. "Yes."

He allowed Robin to steer him toward the doorway. The Hob thrust Shane's coat in his hands. He blinked down at it, not really seeing it at all. "I have to go."

"Yes, you do." Robin led him out the front door, the cold no bother for the Hob. The chill wind plastered the caramel-colored silk shirt to his skin but Robin didn't even shiver. He watched silently as Shane made his way to his studio, those sharp blue eyes catching everything Shane did.

Once inside the building, Shane turned to face him. "Thank you."

"You are most welcome." Robin looked around, curiosity in his gaze. "May I look around?"

Shane nodded, already changing into his coveralls, his vision overriding everything else, even common courtesy. It would be a while before he emerged again, and he'd be more than exhausted when he was done.

Worst of all, when it was over he'd need to call the Seer. If what he was seeing was correct, the world was in for one hell of a ride.

Robin Goodfellow perched on a rafter and looked down on Shane Joloun Dunne. He'd been around those with the Sight often enough to know a vision trance when he saw one, but what surprised him was the way Shane went about bringing his visions to life. The man's hair gleamed with sweat as he worked the forge, purifying silver ore, bending brass and copper to his will. His hands were steady, his touch strong yet delicate as he took glass and molded it, twisted it until he was finally satisfied with shape and hue. His eyes had been, and still were, clouded with visions. Despite that, he'd looked at Robin as if seeing into the Hob without the terror Robin often encountered. If Robin were inclined toward men, it would be such a one who might win his empty, lonely heart.

But Robin knew himself well. Even while wearing the form of a female he was, deep down, a lover of all things feminine. The thought of taking a male lover was, while not exactly repulsive, something that simply did not occur to him. Robin longed for soft, feminine flesh and warm, loving hands. Hands that would caress him, ease the burden on his weary soul. He desired eyes that would see into him without fear, a mind willing to know him, accept him for everything he was. All he wished from life was a soft place to land, a gentle touch, and an acceptance that was beyond most. To find such a thing would be wondrous indeed.

He smiled as he watched the eldest Dunne child through bright eyes. Leo Dunne had found such a one, and little Ruby was a delight to the Hob's heart. She greeted him with glee, hugged him in welcome, and offered him that safe, soft place he yearned for. Had she not been truebonded, he might have been tempted to steal her from the Sidhe lord. But alas, Ruby was forever beyond him, bound by ties of love, soul mated to the man the gods had decreed was hers and hers alone.

And Robin was happy for them. To know such a woman existed and had found her fae mate gave him a hope he'd long since given up on.

Robin held himself perfectly still as Shane sighed wearily. He could tell whatever visions drove the man had almost been purged, but Shane, it seemed, had one last thing to do. One last bit to add to one of the sculptures he'd worked madly on all night, driven to near insanity by what only he could see. Robin wasn't sure what the sculptures meant, but Shane did, and Robin was determined to find out what.

All he had to do was wait.

The doorbell pealed, interrupting the story Sean had been telling about the time Shane had gotten into the neighbor's corral and rode one of the orneriest horses known to mankind. Once he'd been picked up from the dust, he'd told his father he'd known he could ride it, but he hadn't known for how *long*.

From the stories Sean told, Akane was surprised Shane had made it to adulthood. The man was certifiable.

Duncan waved languidly, mellowed by good food and wine. "I'll get it." He opened the door, and all traces of relaxation left him. Jaden went on point, shoving Moira behind him. The chilly smile on Duncan's face was far from welcoming as he greeted his cousin. "Henri. What a lovely surprise."

Akane twisted, startled to see Henri Malmayne at the front door of the Dunne's home. Wasn't he supposed to be in New York? She nodded to him cautiously. Shit, this could blow her cover wide open. "Henri."

Henri nodded, those sharp blue eyes of his taking in everything from the birthday banner to the cake in Akane's hand. "Am I interrupting?"

Jaden shrugged, the smart-ass smirk he so loved to use crossing his face. "Yup. My partner's birthday party. You're not invited."

Henri didn't react to Jaden at all, ignoring the vampire. His attention remained focused on Duncan and Sean Dunne. "I would like to speak with Leo, if you don't mind."

The earth trembled. Sean stepped up to stand beside Duncan, blocking Henri's view of the room. "I don't think so."

"I assure you I mean him no harm."

"Get off my land."

Akane glanced out the window and had to stifle a gasp. The pebbles and dirt that made up the driveway of the Dunne farmhouse were dancing like water on a hot skillet.

Henri held up his hands. "It's to our mutual benefit that Leo comply with our requests. I assure you, I am not my predecessors. I wish to negotiate a compromise rather than force the issue."

"I'm truebonded, Henri. That leaves no room for compromise, I'm afraid." Leo tugged until Ruby was safe under his arm. "There's no way I'll accept a second mate."

Henri sighed. "Perhaps a meeting could be arranged between you and Constance? If you meet, the three of you, perhaps you'll see that what we propose isn't quite as bad as Cullen and Charles made it appear."

Oh *hell* to the no. There was no way Akane was going to allow Leo and Ruby to be alone with a Malmayne. She didn't count Duncan; Duncan was now a Blackthorn thanks to Jaden bonding with both Duncan and Moira before the Sidhe bond took effect. "Only if Jaden and I go with them."

Henri looked pained. "I'm afraid the vampire is not welcome in our home, but we may be able to arrange something where you are present." He turned back to Leo. "Would such an arrangement be acceptable?"

"No." Aileen Dunne stepped forward, tiny and fierce. "The marriage contract has been fulfilled by my daughter. You no longer have any say or sway over my children. Go. Away."

Somehow, the front door closed with no one touching it. Akane blinked. What the fuck?

"How... Who did that?" Duncan looked as startled as everyone else.

Everyone except Jaden, who raised his hand with a wicked grin. "Mea culpa. Sue me, but he was uglifying the place."

Akane choked back a laugh. "Uglifying? Is that even a word?"

Jaden waved at Duncan. "According to him, I'm a lord now and can do whatever the fuck I want. Therefore, I declare Henri Malmayne to be one uglifying bastard." He held out his hand to Moira. "Cake me."

Jaden picked frosting out of his eyebrows with a grimace. Had he truly expected any other response from his fiery mate?

Duncan ran his finger down Jaden's shirt and licked off the frosting. "Mm. Chocolate."

Akane stepped into Shane's studio bright and early the next morning and peered around the vast space. He'd had a corrugated metal building erected where an old corn silo used to stand. Metal and glass working tools littered the space. In the back she could see a doorway cracked open. Shane was nowhere to be seen. Aileen had kept her from coming out here all night despite the strange look on Shane's face as he'd left her birthday party. The fact that he was accompanied by the Hob had made her anxiety even worse. Had Robin recruited Shane? Just the thought had cold shivers running down her spine. "Shane? Are you in here?"

"Back here."

His voice echoed wearily through the metal building, but

she followed his scent until she found him. She stepped through an open doorway to find Shane, his head resting on an empty pedestal, staring at one of his sculptures. He was covered in metal and glass shavings, his coveralls ripped in places, his hands bleeding sluggishly. He looked bemused, exhausted. Beautiful. She approached him like she would a startled fawn, knowing one wrong move might send him running, or worse. If he collapsed would she be able to move him to safety? "Shane? What's wrong?"

"C'mere and tell me what you see."

Her brows rose but she did as asked, moving to stand beside him. Her breath caught.

On the opposite pedestal from where he stood was a metal and glass sculpture, one that sent a shiver of fear through her. It was a ball made out of razor sharp, mirror-like metallic strips, with bits of jagged glass dotting them. The cutting metal edges stuck randomly out into space, creating a chaotic feel that gave Akane the willies. Through the metal strips she could see a tiny figure standing, arms raised like a supplicant, one hand to her chest, one to the sky. "What the hell is that?"

Shane took a deep breath. "What do you *see*?"

She glared at him before taking a closer look. It wasn't until she was almost nose to sharp edge with it did she realize that, inside the ball, the curves were smooth, glistening, reflecting the figure inside over and over again. The face of the figure was serene, if vague in its features, as if Shane couldn't quite see the person's face well enough to sculpt it. "Whatever this ball is, it's protecting the person inside."

"Yeah. I thought you'd see that too."

She shook her head. "What does this mean?"

He lifted his head wearily. His eyes were bloodshot. He must have been up all night working on this. "Follow me." He led her over to another pedestal. "See this?"

"Yeah." It was magnificent, but whereas the last sculpture sent shivers down her spine this one evoked a sense of loss and loneliness. A lone figure stood in shining silver, head bowed, shoulders bent. Flowing down its back, a long sweep of metal she presumed to be the figure's hair crossed over the figure until the tips blended into glass and metal waves. The "foam" of the broken waves brushed the feet of the figure, and how Shane had gotten that effect she had no idea. The figure had no face, but even without it was obvious something dear had been lost, maybe never to be found again. One glistening hand reached toward the waves, either tossing something away or summoning something back. "What are you calling this one?"

"Incomplete."

She blew out a breath. "Wow. Hell of a name."

He chuckled. "No. I mean it's not complete. The rest of the vision hasn't come to me."

Vision? What was he talking about?

He pointed to a small spot in the middle of the sculpture. "Right here. Something is supposed to go right here, but I don't know who or what yet."

Things finally clicked into place. How he'd known where she was going to be the night before, if not why. How he'd known who she was even before she set foot on his father's land. "You have seer's blood in you." It was rare to find, rarer still not to find an accompanying madness underneath. Her mother's people hadn't exactly been prolific before they were wiped away in the war that split the Courts.

Those sapphire eyes, bloodshot though they were, pierced through her. "Where, and on what side, I don't know, but yeah." He shoved a filthy hand through his hair, dislodging what had to be more glass dust. "I finished the ball one last night, but this one has been plaguing me for a while now. Until I know what goes in the center, it remains incomplete."

She turned her attention back to the glass and metal ball. "What do you call that one?"

"What would you call it?"

Dear gods, she did not want to name who it was. Shane didn't just create art. He created *people,* their essence flowing through the piece with shattering results. "Please don't make me."

His hand reached out to her, but he pulled back. "You know, Akane."

She walked back to the jagged ball. "Do you know who she is?"

"Are you so sure it's a she? It could be Oberon."

She shook her head. "I know who this is, and I know what that figure represents. It's a she." She pointed back to the forlorn figure. "Just like I know who that is." She shivered. "You're playing with dangerous visions, Shane."

"Playing? Like I have a choice in this? Unlike you, I don't get to pick and choose what visions come to me. I just get to watch them come alive under my hands." The water in his tiny bathroom started up, and it wasn't long before a pair of damp arms circled her waist. "Akane. Do you know what happens if the figure falls?"

She closed her eyes, but when she opened them, somehow Shane had toppled the figure. Thanks to the way he'd constructed the ball, now the inside only reflected the jagged edges of the outside over and over until there was nothing left but chaos and death. The position of the figure's arms when standing were perfect for a figure lying on the ground as well, and if that happened the world itself would be in danger. "Shit."

"Yeah."

"We should tell Robin."

He turned her around, his big hands gentle. "Can you take a look for me? Maybe I'm missing something." His eyes strayed back to the fallen figure before spearing into her once more. "If this can be avoided, it has to be."

She sighed. "Do you know what happened the last time I tried to get a look at *him*?"

"No, what?"

She leaned against him, trusting him with her weight, for once not caring that her clothes would be covered in grime. She needed his strength after seeing those two pieces of art. "Once, a long time ago, I saw my mother talking to a pretty, pretty man." His arms tightened and she wriggled in protest, turning once more to study the jagged ball. "So I wondered who that pretty man was, but my mother refused to tell me. So I opened my vision, because damn if someone was going to tell me that I couldn't know something." She ignored his belly laugh. "When I woke up, Robin Goodfellow—"

"Who was the pretty man, I presume?"

"Yup. He offered me a job."

"Because he likes that kind of crazy, huh?"

She elbowed him, pleased when he gave a soft grunt. "Do you know who she is?"

"No, and that scares the shit out of me."

"Why?"

"We can't protect her if we don't." He touched one of the jagged edges, his blood welling up, red on silver. "If we don't know…"

"The world will be awash in blood."

"I think so." His hand returned to her waist, cuddling her close. "I think this might be the one thing that could drive him to do something that would make Tunguska look like a cherry bomb."

"Wonderful." The 1908 explosion over the Tunguska region of Russia was had been horrific in its destruction. Scientists believed a meteor or comet fragment exploded roughly three miles above the spot that had been decimated, but there was no solid proof of what had happened. It had the impact of roughly ten to fifteen megatons of TNT. Nothing had survived intact. The fallout from that explosion was seen around the world. Strange light could be seen as far away as England, where people reported that it was bright enough to read the newspaper by. When an expedition was finally sent by the Russians in 1927, the pictures of the devastation had been humbling. And she knew for a fact the scientists had it wrong. No meteor had done that. Robin had, and to this day only two people knew why: High King Oberon and Robin himself. "We need to find out, then."

"I'm thinking of calling your mother."

She winced. "Please don't."

"She's helped me before, when I couldn't interpret a vision. How do you think I got her number?"

She sagged in his arms. "Please not my mom. Please?"

He picked her up like she actually was the dainty little human most people believed she was. His strength never ceased to amaze her...or turn her on. "Man up, Akane. World-wide destruction or talk to your mother." When she didn't answer right away, he shook her.

"What? I'm thinking about it."

With a hearty laugh he carted her out of the studio and back to the tiny attached bedroom, her muttered curses drifting on the air around them.

A glowing pair of green eyes appeared next to one of the pedestals. They stared at the lone figure, waves lapping at its feet, before turning to the jagged ball of glass and metal. A black boot heel clacked on the concrete floor, and Robin Goodfellow materialized out of the nothingness to stare at the fallen figure. The words of the two hybrids echoed in his ears.

"Interesting."

He lifted the small figure with a gentle touch and set it back on its feet. He caressed the side of that serene face with wonder, the metal and glass bending away from him to allow him the simple touch. He smiled, full of hope and anticipation the likes of which he hadn't experienced in centuries. "I wonder who *you* are?"

Chapter Three

"Please."

Akane rolled her eyes. He wasn't going to give up, and she was beginning to understand that she really didn't want him to. Still, it wouldn't do to give in too easily. "Nope."

Bleary blue eyes begged her to give in. "Please. I need."

She sighed. "Fine." Akane allowed some of her inner fire to seep below her skin, the pale human flesh taking on a reddish glow. "Lay down, and don't say a single word."

"But—"

"Ah!"

"But—"

"Shane."

He pouted like a sulky, sick child. "Fine." He flopped down face first on the bed, his broad, naked back daring her to lay hands on it. "Just...please."

He'd showered once they'd reached the bedroom, removing the metal and glass from his hair and skin, changing into nothing more than a clean pair of silk boxer briefs that hugged every inch of him. His body was on display for her, his finest work of art, but he was so exhausted neither of them could truly appreciate it. His muscles were sore, burning from work at the forge, and he'd begged her for a massage.

Akane agreed only after acres and acres of prime real estate had walked out of his bathroom in nothing but his underwear. Damn, the man was fine.

She delicately perched on his ass and placed her hot hands right between his shoulder blades. His groan of appreciation was low and deep, sending shivers through her. Gods, she wanted this amazing man more and more all the time.

What was she going to do? If she allowed Shane any more leeway he'd truly Claim her. His Sidhe half would demand it the moment they had sex, and she wasn't certain it was something he could prevent. Once Claimed, it wouldn't be long before he spoke the Vows that would complete everything, Binding him to her through a display of power and ferocity only the Sidhe seemed to possess. Bands of light would surround him, lethal to any who dared approach him save his chosen mate. He'd speak the Vows, and once done, those bands of light would spear into her, binding their life forces together for all eternity. She'd watched as Duncan and Moira spoke their Vows to Jaden, gasped in delighted wonder at the display of power the two exposed in front of the entire Gray Court. Oberon himself had been there, a cold, perfect otherness that was in direct contrast to the warmth and love that surrounded the new Malmayne-Blackthorns.

And now, if something happened to Jaden, Duncan and Moira would die, forever lost to the world as their souls yearned for something they could never touch again.

She didn't want that for Shane. She didn't want that bright, beautiful spark extinguished, his light lost to the world forever. But being a Blade, and one of Robin's hand-picked assassins, meant she could be killed at any moment, dragging the bound Shane with her into the abyss.

"It's too late, you know."

"Shh." She began kneading his shoulders, letting her warmth seep into him. His voice was slurred, not far from the sleep she needed him to have. He was exhausted to the bone.

"The Claiming has begun. If you try to leave me, I'll get mate sickness."

Her hands paused. "What?"

His shoulders shook. The son of a bitch was laughing at her. "It's too late. It was too late long before our lips touched, but now that they have?" He shrugged, the movement wiggling her where she was seated on his butt. "I *know* I'll develop mate sickness if you disappear on me."

"I thought that only happened if we have sex."

One bleary eye opened long enough to wink at her. "Oh, we will have sex. Trust me." His eye closed again. "But I've tasted you. I know, beyond a shadow of any doubts you might still have, that you're my mate." He shivered under her. "Please, Akane."

Her hands began to move once more, her brain going a mile a minute. "I thought Claiming occurred *after* sex."

"So did Duncan and Moira, but they both got mate sickness after Jaden left. Hate to tell you this, love, but all it takes is a single kiss."

"Shit."

His shoulders tensed. She dug her thumbs into a particularly bad knot, smiling when he gasped. "It's not like I asked you to eat asparagus every day for the rest of your life, you know."

She shuddered. "How did you know I hate asparagus?"

"When Da offered you some you acted like you'd smelled a seriously nasty fart."

She chuckled. "Well, at least you don't smell like

asparagus."

"Don't taste like it, either."

She might have taken that as an invitation if he hadn't sounded so sleepy. She felt safe telling him at least part of her fear. "I don't want anything to happen to you."

"Ditto." He snuggled down into the bedding, nearly asleep. "I'm a lover, not a fighter."

She snorted another laugh. "Go to sleep, Jethro."

"Mm. Akane." And with that, his breathing evened out, her name a soft sigh on his lips.

She gingerly lifted her hands from his skin, unwilling to wake him now that he was finally asleep. "I'm in big trouble." She couldn't stop herself. She curled up next to him, her body heat high for her chilled man, and guarded her greatest treasure as he slept.

Something warm was cuddled up to his back. Shane could feel the heat pouring off the animal and sighed. Sal had crawled into bed with him once again. How the salamander managed to get into his studio he'd never know, but it wasn't the first time and he doubted it would be the last. "Fucking animal."

The bed shifted, and Sal leaned over him, panting heavily. "Woof."

Shane froze. He opened his eyes to find the kind of tongue he wouldn't mind having all over him lolling out of a mouth he was already addicted to. The heat had been Akane, not the salamander. "Good morning, *a ghrá*."

Akane sat back, looking astonishingly prim despite her tangled curls. "What does that mean?"

Shane stretched all over, curling his toes in pleasure. It was nice feeling, waking up to the woman of your dreams.

"What do you think it means?" He stared up at her, daring her to admit she already had the answer.

Her brow furrowed. "I have no clue. I'm a New Yorker, remember?"

He chuckled. "In that case, do you really want the answer?"

She opened her mouth, but something about the look on his face must have stopped her from giving the automatic response she'd intended. "I don't know. Do I?"

He cupped her cheek, running his thumb across those kissable lips. "If I were you, I would."

One brow rose arrogantly. "Good thing I'm not you."

He pulled her down for a good-morning kiss, enjoying the cinnamon and spice taste that exploded on his tongue. God, the woman tasted incredible. "Good morning." He let go and waited for her to run for it.

She cleared her throat, her expression dazed. "Um. Yeah." She shivered delicately. "I have to go to work."

She started to crawl out of bed and Shane bit back a grin. "Break some legs."

She paused. "You did not just say that."

"What?" He grabbed hold of her wrist, feeling the rapid beat of her heart through the delicate skin.

She shook her head and pulled on her arm half-heartedly. She was learning. "Seriously. Ruby's in danger. I have work to do, damn it."

He'd expected more rage from her, but her protest was weak, her tone more thoughtful than pissed. "I would never endanger Ruby or try and stop you from working. You know that."

"Do I?"

There was an old pain under her words, a wound he

intended to lance before it festered any further. The first step was to let go of her wrist and settle back down under the covers. "If you tell me you need to work, then you go." He leaned over and pressed a soft kiss to her jean-clad thigh. "Just remember to come home to me." Shane put his head back down on the pillow and closed his eyes. There wasn't much more he could do at this point in the game short of dragging her down and finishing the Claiming. If he did that, he'd break the fragile trust she'd given him the night before.

He was rewarded by the soft brush of her hand through his hair. "You're a pain in my ass, you know that?"

The affection in the insult was unmistakable. Shane hid his glee behind a warm smile. "I try."

She snorted a laugh. "Where will I be able to find you later?"

"Hither and yon."

"Shane."

He sighed. "If I'm not in my studio I'll be around the farm, helping Dad." He opened one eye and glared at her. "Did you erase my cell phone number again?"

Her big eyes widened, the innocent act lost on him. "It was an accident, I swear."

He rattled off the number and waited for her to input it. "You call me if you need to find me. Even if I'm working I'll answer."

"I'm almost afraid to ask, but how will you know it's me?"

He gestured vaguely toward the floor, his eyes still closed. "Dig my cell phone out of my jeans." He waited until the cold plastic hit his palm before opening his eyes. He had to see the expression on her face for this one. "Now call me."

She did, and when the ring tone sounded she shot off the

bed like it had bitten her. "'Puff the Magic Dragon'? You fucker!"

He started to laugh.

"That's not fucking funny, Shane!" She began beating him with a pillow so hard the thing burst, sending feathers flying in the air. Still he laughed. "You son of a bitch."

He couldn't take her seriously when she was also on the verge of giggles. He rolled his eyes at her and pressed some buttons on his cell. "Fine. Try calling me now, you picky wench."

She picked up her cell phone and dialed again, her brows rising in surprise. "Des'ree's 'You Gotta Be'?"

"Do you have an objection?" He sniffed, sneezing when feather fluff got up his nose. "I preferred 'Puff' myself."

She was still biting back her giggles. "I'm terrified to know what Robin's ring tone is."

"'Welcome to the Jungle'."

She blinked. "Oddly appropriate."

"We got fun and games." He put his arms behind his head and smirked. "Wanna know Oberon's?"

Akane's jaw dropped. "You do not have Oberon's cell number."

"Oh?"

She tried to snatch his phone away but he put it under his pillow before she could. She sniffed. "I knew you were lying."

His brows rose and he pulled his phone out. He held it up so she could clearly see the name and numbers listed.

"Holy shit." Her butt hit the edge of the bed. "How did you get those numbers?"

He shrugged. "I did some artwork for the Gray Palace."

Her shoulders slumped. "Of course you did." She grabbed

the phone out of his hand, choking when she read the name of the song he'd assigned as the High King's the ring tone. "Bruce Springsteen's 'The Iceman'." She cradled his cell in her hand, her gaze glued to his face. "Interesting choice."

"Interesting man." Shane could see the star of her left eye contract and expand. He hid his panic. He could just imagine what would happen if she snuck a peek at the High King. "I wouldn't if I were you. If looking at Robin knocked you out for a week, what do you think checking out Oberon would do to you?"

"Damn it." She flung his cell phone back on his bed and flopped back and across his legs. "Poo."

He laughed softly. "Nobody lets you have any fun, huh?"

"Oh yeah. I haven't killed a Black Court asshole in..." She held up one hand as if counting. "Days."

"Gods above, a bored dragon. Whatever shall I do?"

She reached out and smacked him in the stomach. "Let me get to work, you sneaky bastard."

"Hey now. My parents are married, thank you."

Akane rolled her eyes and stood. Her hands swept through her hair, settling the black, curly mass around her. "Shane?"

"Hmm?" He was awake now, the visions gone, worked out in glass and metal the night before. He could use a cup of coffee and a taste of the woman standing at the end of the bed, idly playing with his footboard.

"Thanks. For my party." She darted a quick glace from under her lashes. "Even if you ditched early."

Pleasure curled through him, better than any sex he'd had with anyone else. He'd given her a taste of what life could be like if she accepted him, and she'd liked it. "You're welcome."

A shy smile darted across her face before she dashed from

the room with an evil laugh. "Coffee's all mine, Farm Boy!" The door slammed shut behind her with a bang, but not before she cried out "COLD!" The door opened and shut much quieter the second time. He assumed she'd reached back in and grabbed her coat.

Shane curled back up in bed and snickered. It would be better all around if he waited to make his way to the main house until after he could wipe away the smug smile on his face.

Akane caught Tristan's attention with ease. The diner she'd gone to was near Henri Malmayne's estate, so she wasn't surprised to find that he wasn't the only Malmayne Sidhe eating there. She was surprised to find that he had a number of what she was calling the Malmayne Malcontents with him.

Whispers had reached her ears that some of the Malmayne clan had begun asking questions about the Gray Court. Whether they'd made similar inquiries about alternate clans within the White she didn't know, but found it an interesting development nonetheless. Most of the Malcontents seemed to be young, below a hundred years old and, surprisingly, each and every one appeared to defer to Tristan.

Fascinating.

Tristan finished up his business and waved away the posse of young Sidhe. He headed for her table with a smile. "Hello again."

She gave him her most flirtatious smile. "Hello to you too, handsome." She waved toward the empty seat across from her. "Care to join me?"

Behind her Etienne fidgeted on his pleather stool, their signal that he was aware the target had been hooked. Now all she had to do was reel him in.

She leaned forward, resting her chin on her palm, and studied him. He was gorgeous, she had to give him that, but he held none of the hot fire Shane did. This man would burn with cold flames much like his cousin Duncan did until someone came and warmed him from the outside. "We never did introduce ourselves." She lifted her head and held out her hand. "Akane Russo." They'd agreed she wouldn't lie to him. If he'd seen her on that video he'd know who she was anyway.

He hesitated a moment before holding out his hand. Perhaps he hadn't seen her after all. "Tristan Malmayne." He gave her a puzzled frown. "May I ask why a Blade would still be in Nebraska?"

She grinned. "My partner is living here now, so I'm back for a visit."

There was a flicker of something in his eyes that she didn't quite catch before it was gone. "I see."

The star in her iris widened as Akane opened her inner sight. She could see the power swirling around him and realized he was much older than he looked. Conflict swirled around him, some dark, some light, mingling at the center into gray. Figures danced within the mist, writhing and gesturing, anger and confusion rampant. "Jaden Blackthorn. I'm sure you've heard of him."

He leaned back in his chair, his expression closed. "You did roll me last night, didn't you?"

Crap. She put her palm to her chest. "Do I look like a Sidhe?" She allowed a brief puff of smoke to exit her nostrils, enough that he caught it but not enough to get in trouble with the very human wait staff.

His lips slowly curved up in a smile. "A dragon. I can't remember the last time I met one of you." His genuine delight dotted the gloomy mist around him with a happy silver and gold glitter. Some of the darkness around him receded, a figure of a man with glowing red eyes shoved out of the picture. "I'm going to make a wild guess and say your temperament is fiery?" She tried to focus on him while Tristan spoke, but the image faded too quickly for her to latch on to it.

"Good guess." She studied the figures around him, noting faces, expressions, anything that might help protect the Dunnes.

He thanked the waitress for refilling his coffee cup and waited until she'd gone. "You seem different than the woman I saw on the video feed."

"That was business." She ran one finger down the back of his hand and batted her lashes. "This is pleasure."

He relaxed a bit more but she could sense the tension still in him. "Nice to know you find my company a pleasure."

She took a deep breath and prepared to lure her little fishy in. "Want to go some place private? Somewhere we can...talk?" She licked her lips, smiling when his gaze glued itself to her mouth.

"I'd love to, but unfortunately I have other plans." He took hold of her hand. "However, if you would be willing to join me for dinner, I'd be more than willing to discuss...talking...further." He pressed a kiss to her knuckles, an open invitation clear in his eyes.

Akane suppressed a shiver. She didn't like his lips on her skin, the way his finger caressed her palm before letting her go. "It's a date."

She waved as he took his leave. What the fuck was wrong with her? She'd wanted to gag at the feel of Tristan's mouth on her, his breath so close it stirred the fine hairs of her arm. Out of the corner of her eye she glimpsed Etienne leaving the restaurant. She'd wait about fifteen minutes before following him out. They couldn't be seen together, not now that she'd hooked their fish.

Besides, there was still pie left on her plate.

Shane followed his father into the tack room and grabbed one of the leather harnesses that needed repairing. His father could move from one edge of his property to another in the blink of an eye, but Sean Dunne loved horses and rode them simply for the joy of it.

"Why haven't you Claimed her yet?"

Shane studied the harness and gathered what he'd need to repair it. "She's skittish."

"Then you need to break her in."

He shot his father a look before turning the harness in his hands. "She needs a gentle touch."

"She needs to be ridden."

Shane choked on thin air. "I am not discussing this with you."

Sean Dunne frowned. "Why not?" The man could have easily been a model; at four-hundred-and-twenty-five years of age his Seeming still had the looks of a twenty-seven year old human, a gift from his bonding his Sidhe mate. His true appearance was even more stunning. When Sean Dunne allowed his inner leprechaun to show, those sapphire eyes glowed with power. His skin would show the brown whorls of his earthy heritage and his dark hair would grow, landing at shoulder length. The strength of the earth itself flowed in Shane's father, and there was no one he admired more.

But he still wasn't discussing his sex life with the man. "Leave it be, Da."

"No. Not until you tell me why."

"Because you're my father."

Sean snorted in disgust. "Please. Like I don't know what that thing between your legs is begging you to do."

"Da!" Leave it to an earth sprite to get...earthy. Shane pointed the tool he was using at his father and scowled. "Don't make me call Ma."

Sean grinned, completely unrepentant. "You need her. She needs you. Get her ass tipsy and topple her, boy."

Shane was horrified. This was getting worse and worse. "Is that the advice you gave Leo?"

"Nope."

"Why not?"

His father shot him a knowing look. "Because he's not you." Sean dropped the tack back on the scarred work table and took Shane's face between his hands. "Leo is like your mother. Gentle, with a core of strength none can deny. Moira is more like me, willing to fight with all her strength for what's right but able to turn around and admit when she's wrong. And you?"

Shane took a deep breath at the look on his father's face. "What about me?"

"You're the best of us both." His father leaned forward and whispered in his ear. "But don't tell your sister I said that. I don't think I could handle the puppy eyes."

Shane closed his eyes and swallowed. "Thanks, Da."

Sean released him and Shane opened his eyes. "She needs you, Shane. She needs *us*."

"I know." Shane leaned against the table. "Her life before us was cold." He allowed the vision that had driven him to create *Akane* dance behind his eyes. "No room to fly, no place to be free."

Sean scowled, the part that made him such an incredible

father ready to defend his son's mate against all comers. "Her mother didn't abuse her, did she?"

Shane shook his head. "No, not really. She tried her best, but can anyone truly understand the needs of a young dragon but another dragon?" He'd slipped back into his mother's native language, speaking to his father in the Sidhe tongue as they often did when trading secrets. "Her father died to keep the Seer safe, sacrificing himself so she could escape with an infant Akane." Shane swallowed. He could only imagine the Seer's devastation as she'd fled, knowing her mate's fate, and her own. "She knew, Da. She knew when she met him what would happen and loved him anyway."

"There's strength in that."

"Aye. And she's done her best for Akane since, but even the Seer can't see into her heart."

"Can you?"

He sighed. "I'm trying."

"Perhaps you see her better than most."

Shane was pleased that he didn't jump. He was equally pleased that his father did. It served him right after the discomfort of their previous discussion.

Only Robin Goodfellow could sneak up on a leprechaun on his own land. The bond between a leprechaun and the land he laid claim to was incredibly strong. Sean could sense every single person on it, hear whispers a mile away, open holes in the ground barely a pin wide that went all the way to the core of the earth. It took a minor deity to sneak up on him on a *bad* day.

Robin did it without even trying.

"Good day, Robin."

The redheaded menace stepped into the tack room wearing

the gaudiest western shirt Shane had ever seen. If he stepped into any straight bar in Nebraska every redneck for miles would try and kick his ass for that shirt alone. Add in the super tight jeans, the shiny alligator boots and the black cowboy hat with the purple-checked bandana for a band, and you had one fey-looking fae. "And good day to you, Shane Dunne." Robin leaned against the door jamb, his arms crossed, one toe digging into the scratched wooden floor. "Akane giving you fits?"

Shane eyed the Hob's outfit. "Is this your way of telling me I should giddy-up?"

Robin grinned and pulled something out of thin air. The silver and gold object glittered in the light, the intricate lines and swirls etched in it as familiar as Shane's own skin. "I think you understand her quite well."

"I didn't get a chance to give that to her last night."

"Does she know what the prize inside is?"

"No, and I'm not planning on telling her either." He grinned. "That's half the fun, isn't it?"

Robin laughed easily and tossed the puzzle box to him. Shane caught it easily. "She's meeting Tristan Malmayne for dinner tonight." He held up his hand at Shane's rumble of discontent. "Let it go. Trust her, if not me. No harm shall come to your mate this eve."

Shane ran his hands through his hair. It would be hard to stay away from her knowing she was with another man. A man who'd touched her skin, embraced her warm body. "I'll do my best."

"Good. Because this is part of who she is, and if you try to take that from her, your little bird will fly away."

Leaving Shane to rot in the grief of mate sickness. "I understand." He darted a glance at his silent father before turning his attention back to Robin. "Did you see it?"

75

That eerie flash of green erupted from Robin's eyes. "Yes."

"Did you understand it?"

Robin grinned, and Shane shivered. "*Yes.*"

The purring anticipation in Robin's voice warned him to keep any misgivings to himself.

"You've had a vision?"

Shane turned to his father, nothing but acceptance on the other man's face. "Aye."

Sean nodded once and turned to the Hob. "You've helped our family after the debt was paid. If you need us, call."

The Hob's eyes went wide and dark, the awful, yawning emptiness Shane had seen in him lightening just a hair. "Thank you, Sean Dunne of Clan Blackthorn."

Somehow, that thanks sounded more like a vow.

Shane had never been prouder of his father.

Robin's attention turned once more to Shane, that wicked grin once more on his lips, the moment lost forever. "Well? What are you going to do about Akane? Hmm?"

Shane snatched Robin's hat and plunked it on his own head. "Giddy-up." He tossed the puzzle box back to Robin, winking at his father while Robin's laughter filled the barn.

Chapter Four

Akane sat in the restaurant and waited for her date to show up. She'd texted Shane a message letting him know she'd be late getting home that evening and reminding him to stay close to the farm where Sean could protect him. His *Yes, dear* had not amused her.

Not much, anyway.

She wiped the silly smile off her face and glanced once more at the restaurant door, nodding when her date walked in. She'd used the excuse of wanting her own car and first-date jitters to get out of having him pick her up. If Tristan figured out she was staying with the Dunnes rather than Jaden no lie would save her. She'd be forced to take drastic measures.

"You look amazing." Tristan brushed a kiss across the top of her head before sitting across from the table.

She couldn't help the little zing of pleasure at the compliment even as her skin crawled at the caress. "Thank you." She held up her glass. "I took the liberty of ordering our wine. I hope you don't mind."

There was the slightest tightening around his eyes. "Not at all."

Liar. This was a man who enjoyed ordering for a female. If she'd known she would have held off on the wine. She decided to stroke his manly ego a touch. "I can't believe you found a place like this out in the boonies." She looked around, allowing her approval to shine through. She had to drag Shane here at some point whether he liked it or not.

Tristan leaned back in his chair with a smug expression. "It is a good find, isn't it? A friend of mine suggested it might be a nice place to take a beautiful lady."

Akane toyed with her fork and shot him a flirtatious look. "How many ladies have you brought then?"

"Several. But none as beautiful as you." Tristan lifted his glass and toasted her silently.

Gag. Me. Akane toasted him back and sipped her Bordeaux, enjoying the full, bold flavor bursting across her tongue. She bet Jethro would hate it.

Out of the corner of her eye she caught a flash of blonde hair. She kept her gaze on Tristan, but allowed her inner sight to open.

Constance Malmayne was leaving the restaurant. Not surprising, since the food here was up to even the Malmayne's exacting standards. What was surprising was the fierce expression on her face as she spoke into her cell phone. Akane couldn't hear her words, but her tone came through loud and clear. Constance was pissed off at whoever was on the other end of the phone, and Akane had the urge to run across the room and "accidentally" bump into the woman to find out who she was speaking with.

"Akane?"

She turned her attention back to Tristan. Whatever Constance was up to would have to wait. Akane had a bigger fish to land.

They made small talk as they waited for their food, the soft sounds of cutlery on china the only music. After they'd eaten Akane suggested dessert. There was a hell of a lot of flirting she could do over chocolate mousse.

Tristan agreed, and Akane proceeded to seduce him into a stupor. She ran her tongue slowly across the back of the spoon to catch every last bit of deep, rich chocolate. She swirled her finger through the whipped cream, making sure to suck it off in a gesture just this shy of obscene. Licking chocolate off her lips earned her a soft groan, and when she "accidentally" ran her foot down his calf Tristan asked her back to his room.

Once there, she'd get what she needed and get out, leaving Tristan with a memory that would rock him for years to come. One of the perks of having a Sidhe for a partner was their ability to weave a believable fantasy for someone simply by dipping into their mind. The recipient of the fantasy would have all of their senses immersed in it, making it seem like reality. Most Sidhe used this ability to protect themselves from humans or weave romantic fantasies for lovers.

Sidhe Blades used it to mine information from unsuspecting targets. Etienne would ensure that Tristan fully believed Akane had pleasured him into a stupor before slipping away into the night.

She let him place his hand at the small of her back as they walked out of the restaurant. All of Akane's appetites had been sated. Tristan's were still on the edge. "So I'll follow you back to your place?"

"No need. I think we can take one car, don't you?"

Something about the way Tristan said it had her dragon senses tingling. The Sidhe was up to no good, and getting in his car would be a mistake. "Oh, but I wanted to make sure I still had my car, remember?"

Tristan tipped her face up. "Trust me. It won't be necessary."

That sounded strangely like a threat. Akane gripped his

wrist and pushed his hand away, much to his shock. "Oh, I think it will."

When he shoved her back she nearly fell. "That's too bad. I was looking forward to tonight."

For some reason she wasn't surprised when the weapons came out, two silver blades finely honed to a wicked edge. "Nice." She whipped out her own blade and kicked off her heels. "Bad spot for this, though. Wouldn't do to let the local yokels get a look."

"At these? Hell, around here they're pocket knives." He slashed out, humming happily when she dodged out of his way. "God, you are the hottest thing on two legs."

"Should I try for four?"

"Even these people aren't *that* blind, sweetheart." He lunged, attempting to disarm her, his off-hand blade shielding him.

Akane blocked his blow and swiped at his face with *her* off hand, her black claws drawing blood. "Oopsie. Tristan gots a boo-boo."

"So does Etienne."

Their swords clashed together, the sound strangely muffled. Tristan had to be hiding them from the humans coming and going from the restaurant. It was the only explanation.

Hell, if he wanted to tire himself out on illusions who was she to argue?

She glared at him. "What did you do to Etienne?"

"Nothing permanent. Yet." He slashed at her side, drawing a thin, bloody line through her favorite shirt. "Who do you work for?"

"Robin Goodfellow. And you? Seen *Her* recently, you Black

Court son of a bitch?"

His swords faltered for a moment before he clumsily blocked her blow. "The Dark Queen does not know my face. Can the same be said for yours?"

She slashed at him, driving him back a step. "Puh-lease. Have you met anyone of the Black Court who'd dare say Robin's name?"

"Say it, yes. But will they sing it?"

As she blinked in shock he disarmed her. The point of his blade rested against her throat. "Sing, little dragon."

Akane saw red. Her hair lifted off her neck, forming her dragon's ruff. Her horns pierced through the midnight strands. It was time to break out the big guns. "Eat shit and die, tapeworm."

"Fuck." Tristan thrust at her throat but it was too late. Akane had shifted. The blade bounced harmlessly off her hide.

Akane bared her fangs at the pale Sidhe. "You were saying?"

Tristan dropped his sword and put his hands behind his head. They were useless against her now, and he must know that. "Just so you know I'm not the only one she sent."

"Who else?"

He scowled. "No fucking way I'm giving up my partner to you, scum."

"Scum? I'm not the one working for the Black, asshole!" Akane's head tilted. "Well." She sat on her haunches and lifted her back paw, absently scratching an itch behind her ear. "Damn. You work for Glorianna, don't you?"

Tristan eyed her curiously. "Are you that limber in your human form?"

Akane's paw dropped. "Don't make me eat you."

He grinned.

"In the you-are-crunchy-and-taste-good-with-ketchup way."

The grin turned wicked. "You are that limber, then." He eyed her, nose to snout. "Can I lower my arms now?"

She puffed out some smoke, holding her amusement when he coughed. "Where's Etienne?"

"The trunk of my car." When she sighed wearily he shrugged and asked, "Where would you have put him?"

Akane shifted back, adjusting her skirt before he got too good a look at the Promised Land. "You do know you shoved a Knight of Oberon in your trunk."

"Prove it."

"Sure." She held up her phone and lit it up. Her finger hovered over the number two. "I have Robin Goodfellow on speed dial."

"Let me dig out my keys."

It didn't take long to get a groggy Etienne out of the trunk of Tristan's car and into the back seat of hers. She dropped him off at the hotel room before following a much quieter Tristan to a secluded spot where, if they fought again, no humans would be accidentally barbecued. Tristan, apparently willing to work with her, even let her car block his on the dirt road.

"I have a peace offering, if you're willing." Tristan held up a bottle of Goldschläger enticingly.

"Dragons don't get drunk." Their bodies burned off the booze way too quickly.

"But you do enjoy a good buzz, don't you?" He shook the bottle. "C'mon. I brought the good stuff. Only the best for my faux dates."

She eyed the bottle warily. Goldschläger didn't contain

enough real gold to give her problems, but he could have tainted the alcohol some other way. "You first."

He twisted off the cap and took a healthy swig. He shuddered and held out the bottle. "Now you."

Akane took the offered bottle and sniffed delicately at the neck, looking for signs of poison. The scent of cinnamon liquor hit her, warm and enticing. She could detect the faintest hint of gold in the bottle and she salivated. Her body damn near vibrated at the metallic scent that permeated the liquid.

Tristan held his arms out to the sides, obviously *not* reaching for some form of antidote. She had no sensation that her senses were being tampered with.

Akane took a swig, shivering as gold-laced fire raced down her throat. "Mmm." She rubbed the bottle against her, almost wishing it was the liquor itself.

"Whoa." Tristan lowered his arms slightly and stepped forward. "Lemme double-check that bottle."

Akane hissed at him, hugging the bottle closer.

"Alrighty then. You just hold that for now, 'kay?" Tristan's hands went back up.

Akane eyed the Sidhe. She didn't trust him. He was going to take her gold away.

As if she'd let him.

Akane lifted the bottle to her lips and proceeded to down it like she was a five-year-old drinking the last glass of sweet tea on a hot summer day.

"Good girl." Tristan lowered his arms and took a step forward. "Maybe I shouldn't tell you this now, but that's not really Goldschläger."

Akane tilted her head. Gods, he was a pretty, pretty man. Moonlight silvered his golden hair, kissed his pale skin.

Something inside her throbbed at the thought of having him between her thighs.

Then the light hit his gray eyes, and Akane blinked. No. This wasn't the pretty man she wanted. This was someone else.

She wanted the pretty man with the sapphire eyes and the smooth, rich voice. That voice alone could make her come if it whispered the right words.

Akane took a step back. "Then what is it?" Arousal tightened her belly, threatened to put her on her back for the wrong person.

"You see, Goldschläger dilutes the gold it puts into its liquor, and that wouldn't do for what I had in mind." Tristan reached out and touched her hair, tugging gently. Akane shook her head, freeing herself. "This is Gold*wasser*. Direct from the original factory." He poked the bottle and earned himself another possessive growl. "The gold in there is twenty-four carat and utterly pure."

Akane blinked. Oh. That would explain a lot.

"Once I figured out you were a dragon, I knew the best way to immobilize you would be to have you drink gold." Tristan stroked his hand down her cheek, blinking when she moaned. "But the effects aren't quite what I had intended. I merely meant to knock you out for a while, not send you into heat. Apparently my research was... insufficient." He took a step back. "Akane?"

She was trembling with want, desperate for touch, even his. "I need."

"I would provide, but I have the feeling you'd hate me in the morning." He smiled sadly. "Besides, you've already been Claimed. If you want this fire doused, you need to find your mate. He's the only one who can ease the heat."

What? "How do you know that?"

"Any Sidhe can see it, sweetheart."

"Don't call me that." Her teeth were chattering, the arousal climbing to painful levels. "I *hurt*."

"Whether you believe it or not, I'm sorry for that. It wasn't my intention, despite how it looks." Tristan leaned against a tree and sighed. She could scent his arousal. He wanted her, but he held up his hand with a look of regret. "Fly home, little bird. There's a warm hand waiting for you to land in."

With a shriek of despair Akane shifted, spread her wings, and flew where she needed to be.

Home.

Shane stretched wearily. Cleaning up the studio always seemed to take forever, and after a day following his father around the farm the last thing he'd wanted to do was come back and sweep up metal shavings and glass shards. But if Akane was going to be coming back here there was no way he'd leave the dangerous pieces around for her to cut herself on.

He put the broom back in the closet and headed for the shower, eager to wash off the dirt of the day. He couldn't wait until his little dragon showed up. He planned on giving her the present he'd made, the puzzle box gleaming all by itself on one of the empty pedestals in the display section of his studio. Akane would adore it, and if he kept slowly reeling her in without scaring her she'd eventually love the prize inside.

A deep, feral growl rumbled through the studio. It bounced off the walls, echoed in the high places. Shane wasn't certain where it came from, but he knew who it was.

It seemed that, for some unknown reason, Akane was seriously pissed at him.

"*A ghrá?*"

A low rumbling sound was his only answer.

"If you tell me what I've done wrong I'll endeavor to fix it." He tipped back the silly cowboy hat he'd stolen from Robin and stared up into the rafters. Was she there, perched, staring down at him?

"Shane."

He whipped around, stunned by the pain in her voice. "Akane."

She stood behind him, panting, arms crossed over her chest. Her horns peeked out of her hair. Her pupils were dilated, the hazel star in her left eye almost obscured. She was trembling hard enough that he feared for her bones.

Shane fought the rage that exploded at the sight. "Who hurt you?"

She took a step toward him and froze. She sniffed deeply. Her head fell back, a look of sheer bliss crossing her face. "Oh yes." A predatory smile lit her face, her gaze focusing on his body. The trembling stopped. Her arms fell to her sides as she tilted her head, watching him, waiting for him to do...something. He could sense the tension in his mate as she inched closer to him. "I need."

Only then did he understand what must have happened. Once he'd realized his mate would be a dragon he'd learned as much as he could about them. "That fucker fed you gold, didn't he?"

Akane nodded, the movement more of a promise than an answer. She crooked her finger at him. The golden star in her left eye glittered dangerously.

"Why, Grandma, what big eyes you have." Shane stepped back a pace. "If you do this, you'll hate me in the morning."

Akane ran her palms across her breasts, and really? That

was so not fair. Shane had been dreaming about what color her nipples might be from the moment he met her. She licked her lips, her fingers inching toward the hem of her shirt.

"Oh, now. Hold on there." Shane held up his hands. "There's got to be another way. Maybe if we put you to sleep we can ride it out until the gold is out of your system."

She shook her head. "Want you." The shirt went flying, and Shane got his first glimpse of her underwear.

White. She'd worn white, sheer lace to a date with another man. Shane could clearly see her nipples now, like warm chocolate kisses had melted on the tips of her breasts. He'd always been a sucker for white lace. "Oh fuck me."

"Good idea." Akane pounced.

"Whoa!" Shane caught her before they both hit the floor. "Okay, *a stór*." Her legs wrapped around his waist, and damn it, those full lips attached themselves to his neck and proceeded to shut down his forebrain. "Um. Yes. Sleeping it off would be…" He shuddered as her talented lips worked themselves down his neck. His cock beat an insistent tattoo against his zipper, eager to get the party started. "Later."

Shane turned and started to carry her to the bedroom, his only thought to see if her panties matched her bra. If they did, he was a dead man. His dragon would devour him, and he'd go happily into *that* good night, thank you.

Shane almost dropped them both to the floor when Akane began dry humping him. Purr-like sounds poured from her throat as she ground against him. Sheer lust killed what little was left of his thoughts. Need rode him hard, the knowledge that his mate was willing in his arms overriding everything else.

Shane dumped her ass on the edge of his work table, the one he used to conjure raw materials. It was clean and bare, and thank the gods he'd done that earlier or she'd have splinters in her ass when he was through with her. He ripped her skirt off, groaning at the sight of the sheer lace, white panties. He gripped her inner thighs and pushed her legs as wide as they would go. He leaned down and licked her through those sheer panties, groaning at the warm taste of his mate. Her flavor burst across his tongue even through the lace.

Akane leaned back and propped her heels on the edge of the table, holding herself spread open. Her toes curled. "Mmm."

Shane could feel his magic flexing, the sparks dancing along his skin. There was no way he could stop himself from completing the Claiming, not if he made love to her. Green and gold sparks lit the room, the light strong enough to dance across Akane's skin. If she was going to object, now had to be the time, while he could still force himself away from her.

When her hips thrust up into his face he took that as consent.

Shane proceeded to lick his mate's pussy with all the fervor of a starving man determined to get every last crumb on his plate. The panties were soon toast, Akane's claws ripping them away so he could get to her unhindered. He spared a single, mourning thought for the pretty lace before he dove back in.

He planned on seeing her in white lace again, the sooner the better.

Akane leaned back and let Shane have his wicked way with her body. His mouth was so good on her, his lips and tongue playing her pussy like a virtuoso. Shane seemed to be one of those men who truly enjoyed eating out his partner, and Akane was the lucky, lucky recipient of his talent.

She purred in pleasure as he took her clit between his lips, stroking it over and over with his tongue until she exploded for him. "More." She sat up and grabbed his head, pulling that talented mouth to her breast. Her core throbbed, wet and needy.

She didn't know if she was going to kill Tristan or kiss him for this.

Shane suckled her through the thin lace bra, turning the lace transparent. He pulled away and traced the wet material with his finger, and damn if he didn't have the most reverent look on his face. "You are so beautiful." His eyes had darkened to near black, his face filled with need.

"Let me see you." If they were going to do this, she wanted all of him. She had no idea what he'd look like, but hybrids like herself and Shane often had an unusual appearance that could freak others out.

Akane had no intention of being freaked, no matter how odd Shane's true appearance was. After all, she was also a hybrid and understood what could happen, the strange way their unique abilities could etch themselves into their skin and bones.

His brows rose, but Shane did what she wanted. He dropped his human Seeming, and she got a look at her man without the filter of his fake humanity. Akane almost swallowed her tongue at her first sight of Shane without his Seeming.

He was gorgeous. The vibrant red-gold hair of his human Seeming seemed dull as dishwater compared to the almost metallic shine of his true appearance, rich as Black Hills gold mixed with copper. His hair grew to just below his shoulders, emphasizing his strong jaw. Those blazing sapphire eyes glittered like dark jewels, the whorls of his leprechaun heritage emphasizing them like pale tribal markings. Light danced around him, gold and green, in a hypnotic pattern, sometimes random, sometimes making figures or places she could almost see. Before she could make sense of them they were gone, lost in the dancing fireworks display around her man. His skin sparkled like it was coated in golden glitter, reflecting the light of his magic back into the room, creating a halo like effect around his body. Even his fingernails glittered with green and gold, as if he'd been carved from the very earth itself and adorned with its finest gems.

"My god," she breathed, taking his face between her palms.

His slow smile took him from gorgeous to breathtaking. It was like he'd been made from her dreams, carved from her deepest desires. There was no way Akane could turn away from him now.

"Now you."

Akane closed her eyes. In her human form, she was cute. Her true appearance, however, left much to be desired. She was nowhere near Shane in looks when she let her inner hybrid out.

"Akane." A kiss brushed across her cheek, scented with her essence. "Let me see you, *a ghrá*."

Akane took a deep breath and dropped her Seeming.

Shane bit back a moan as Akane's hair rose from her neck in an unseen breeze. Most thought dragons were fire or water elementals, but they were wrong. Only those borne of air could fly, and Akane was surrounded by her element. Deep golden horns glittered atop her head. The iris of her eyes widened, ate up the whites until they could barely be seen. The dark brown eye darkened to black, the hazel star in its center lightening to purest, scintillating gold. Her other, more draconic eye matched the golden star in color if not in impact. It was as if that star was truly glowing in the center of her Seer's eye. The gift of her mother's heritage shone with a light of its own, more fascinating than any star Shane had ever seen.

Akane's skin went from lightly tanned to deep gold. Her

hands turned black halfway up her forearms, the deadly claws she'd unsheathed blending in seamlessly. Her fangs poked her full bottom lip, enticing Shane to lick them until she begged for mercy. But best of all those glorious golden wings of hers rose above them both, stretching until they almost touched the ceiling of his studio before settling around his mate like a golden cloak for a dragon queen.

Akane's head tilted, the star in her eye glowing fiercely. "You think I'm beautiful."

Her voice echoed with power, part her mother's heritage, part her father's. Thanks to her powers she could see exactly how he saw her, her golden breasts barely held back by white lace, her deadly claws carefully stroking his back.

Or not. Shredded, his shirt fell from his back, his skin barely marked.

"Want you naked."

Shane covered his privates before she could shred his jeans. "Leave me something to go back to the house in, *a ghrá.*"

"What does that mean?" Her gaze was glued to his cock as he stripped off his jeans.

He palmed himself, grinning mischievously. "It means I want you." She growled at him, and he laughed. "It means my love."

She jerked. "And *a stor?*"

"My darling."

He held still as her wings extended behind him. He could almost taste the panic in her. "It's too soon for love."

He let that pain slide through him. For her, perhaps, it was too soon. He'd been lost the moment he'd seen his own future in metal and glass. He'd have to make her believe it, because Shane Joloun Dunne wasn't going anywhere without Akane

Russo, even if he had to stuff her in an adult-sized baby papoose and cart her around on his back kicking and screaming. He cupped her cheek despite knowing she could easily gut him in this position. "You are *a ghrá mo chroí.*"

"Shane."

"Do you want to know what that means?" He kissed her, the tips of her fangs tickling his tongue. "It means my heart's beloved."

She shuddered. The aphrodisiac was still in her system. Soon it would compel her forward to take him. To Claim him, whether she liked it or not. "You don't know me."

His brows rose. For just an instant his lights created *Akane*, the piece he'd named after her.

Her hand reached out to touch the sparks but they dispersed, *Akane* lost once more to the dance. She whimpered. He wasn't sure if it was because she hadn't been able to touch *Akane* or if the desire had begun to ride her once more. Her wings enfolded him, drawing him closer, and Shane decided it must the aphrodisiac.

He pulled her close, determined to wring every last drop of pleasure he could from her body. If all he could count on to hold her was pleasure, then he'd make sure to deliver it to her in spades.

Akane shivered as Shane's feelings ran through him and into her. The warmth of his love washed over her, settled the jitters Tristan's little present had left her with. She took his hands and placed them on her skin, hoping he'd get the hint.

She was ready for more. Ready to be loved, even if she wasn't quite ready for love herself. She'd greedily gobble up every drop he fed her until they were both sated.

Those artist's fingers traced her skin, kneaded her shoulders, dipped down her waist and caressed her thighs until she was once more trembling and ready to scream. And all the while his mouth devoured hers, his tongue dueling with her own in an age-old dance neither could hope to win. The tip of his tongue caressed her fangs, enticing her to bite. Akane scraped her claws as gently as she could up his sides, smiling into the kiss when he shivered.

Soon her legs were once more wrapped around his waist, but this time they were both gloriously naked. She needed him inside her, dousing the golden flames that danced within her. She tried to pull him toward her, to lure him inside, but Shane resisted. That stubborn strength of his was more than a match for her.

"No. Not here." He lifted her easily and carried her toward the small bedroom. He laid her, careful of her wings, on her back. "How would you like me, *a ghrá?*"

She grinned. It was time to give a little back, to see if the gold sparkling on his skin was as tasty as it looked. Akane sat up and pushed him back until he sat on his heels, his erect cock bobbing up from between his thighs like a tasty treat. She licked her lips and lowered her head.

"You don't have to."

She shot him a disbelieving look.

His cock bobbed against her chin. "But if you want to, I'm totally fine with it."

Akane slowly licked him from the bottom of his cock to top, moaning as his flavor burst across her tongue. Shane tasted divine, all rich salty goodness. She needed more of him, more of his flavor, and she couldn't wait to get it.

She sucked him into her mouth, making sure to use her tongue to lap at him. Her head bobbed up and down his length, her tongue working overtime to bring her mate pleasure.

"Oh. *A ghrá.* Yes, please." He buried his hands in her curls, his fingers brushing her horns. Akane groaned, the sensation of her mate touching her there rocketing through her. Only her mate was allowed that intimate touch.

"You like that, *a ghrá?*" His fingers stroked over her horns again. Akane hummed happily, increasing the suction on Shane's cock so he'd know just how much she liked it.

Shane began to thrust in and out of her mouth, tiny little movements that let her get used to him before he increased his strokes. She let him know when he'd pushed it too far by wrapping her hand around the base of his cock to keep him from choking her. He backed off immediately, giving her horns another stroke in apology.

Akane let him fuck her mouth for a few more moments, debating whether or not she wanted him to come. She was leaning toward yes when strong hands gripped her horns and gently pulled her off his mouth.

Akane whimpered. How the hell did he know the ways dragons mated? He was using her horns in just the right way, stroking them, using them to control her movements.

He was right. They *were* mates. It was the only explanation for the way he instinctively drove her insane.

"I want inside you, Akane. Let me come in."

Akane shuddered with need. His taste had driven her wild, his touches igniting her inner fire until she was ready to burst into flames. But still, this first mating wasn't quite right. Thank the gods she knew how to fix it. She nearly whacked him with her wings as she rolled over and got to her knees, her ass raised in the air.

If he was going to mate a dragon, damn it all, he was going to do it *right.*

"Oh." He caressed her ass, the touch firm. The rough skin of his fingers scrapped across her flesh. "I do like the way you think."

She wiggled her ass. Akane was done with the talking. It was time to get on with the fucking. "Now, Shane."

He gripped her hips. The head of his cock pressed against her opening. "Nag, nag, nag." He began to slide into her, the hot width of him stretching her. "I can see what the rest of our relationship is going to be like."

Akane grinned and batted him with her wings.

"Yup. That's about right." He chuckled breathlessly. "Have I told you yet that you have an amazing ass?"

Akane turned her head, trying to see him behind her. Her wings were in the way, hiding him from view. So Akane did the only thing she could to get this party started. She clenched every muscle she had below her waist.

"Ah." Shane hissed, sounding almost dragon-like. He pulled almost all of the way out, only the head of his cock still inside. "That's not fair."

Akane tilted her hips and drove herself backward, impaling herself. "Nope. Teasing me right now is not fair."

"I'm not a tease, *a ghrá*. I put out." With that Shane set up a punishing rhythm that had her purring like a madwoman. He forced her to practically curl up into a ball so he could curve his body over hers. His hands left her hips to grip her horns, sending Akane into a spiral of pleasure so intense she shrieked, her dragon song echoing through the studio. The orgasm was so strong Akane swore stars danced in the room.

"Again."

"Yes." The grip on her horns kept her on the edge of another orgasm. She never wanted this to end, her golden man fucking her senseless until the only thing left was the blinding pleasure. "Shane. Yes."

"Yes. Come, *a ghrá*. Let me feel you come."

He stroked her horns just right, his grip firm. The tips of his fingers brushed over and over again across the sharp ends until he had to have left behind blood. Akane shrieked again, coming so hard she nearly blacked out.

How the hell did he *know*? Stroking her horns was the equivalent of stroking her clit, except there was more to play with.

Her shoulders dropped wearily to the mattress. She was wrung out, strung up on the high he was forcing from her. "No more, Shane, no more."

"Yes, more. One more, then we can sleep."

His damn hands worked her horns while his cock worked her body. His thrusts began to falter, his body slamming into hers harder. "Soon. Gods, soon, Akane."

She began to climb the sharp cliff of ecstasy one last time. With this, Shane's Claim on her would be complete. All that would be left would be to mark him in her own way, the symbol of her dragon forever etched onto his flesh. "Give me your arm."

Shane let go of one of her horns and put his arm where she could easily reach it. She gripped him tightly as the orgasm spiraled through her. She took that energy and focused it, directed it into his arm before it overwhelmed her. She barely heard his roar of completion, his song complementing hers as together, in a flash of golden light, Shane and Akane became one.

Shane dropped to the mattress, so wrung out he could barely move. He'd never had sex like that in his damn life. If this was what being mated to a dragon was like, he only wished he'd found her sooner. "Akane?"

His only answer was a delicate snore. He stifled his laughter at the sight of his mate, ass still up in the air, passed out from pleasure. "Damn." He adjusted her until her body relaxed into the mattress, covering her with her wings until nothing but her horns and her toes peeked out. It was the perfect living blanket, and he couldn't understand why she didn't sleep like that more often.

Shane stood up and went to the small bathroom, eager to finish his business and crawl back into bed with his newly Claimed fiancée. Now that he'd started the process he'd feel the need to finish the job more and more, giving her the Sidhe Vows and Binding their life forces together for all eternity. He had no doubts that this was a truebond, just like his sister and brother had found.

He switched on the light and blinked. He hadn't realized how dim the light in his bedroom had gotten. He smiled as he glanced back at Akane. He'd have to get a bigger bed. Maybe he'd make the headboard and footboard himself, something dotted with precious gems for his dragon queen to lie on.

He turned to the mirror and lifted his hand to brush his hair back from his eyes. He was always startled to see his true form in the mirror. He'd gotten used to the...look...of...

Shane lowered his arm and stared at the dragon tattooed on the inside of his forearm. It was Akane, golden and dark, wings spread, her tail forming the symbol of infinity. Shane touched the mark and Akane shifted in her sleep.

His brows rose. "Well. What do we have here?" If Shane was a meaner man, he'd play with that tattoo and see what else he could do to his little mate. But Akane had to be exhausted. The gold poisoning mingled with their energetic Claiming meant his dragon would need her sleep.

He'd be a bastard another day, when she wasn't working a case. For now, he'd let his love sleep. He finished his business and crawled back into bed, eager to share the warmth she'd denied him for so long.

Chapter Five

Shane kissed Akane's cheek, eager for his woman to wake up. He had something he wanted to give her, and he was tired of waiting.

One bleary gold eye opened before Akane groaned out a laugh. "Most people kiss the *facial* cheek."

"Where's the fun in that?" Shane plopped down next to her, the puzzle box cupped in his hand. He held out the glittery object. "Happy birthday."

He'd never seen a woman snatch something from him so fast before in his life. "For me?" Those amazing eyes blinked coquettishly, a roguish grin on her lips.

"Yup. Made with my own two hands."

The playfulness departed to be replaced with puzzlement. "You made this? It doesn't look like anything else you've made before." She turned it in her hands. "The line carvings are nice, though."

Damn, she sounded like someone desperately trying to say something nice. "It's a puzzle box."

She stiffened beside him. Her wings fluttered rapidly. "Puzzle box?" She eyed him warily. "Made by you?"

He nodded. "It's pretty intricate. If you like, I can show you how to open it."

She scrambled away from him, puzzle box clenched in her fist. "Mine!"

"Okay." He lay back and put his arms behind his head. "But you need any help, Miz Akane, you come fetch me, y'hear?"

She growled low in her throat. "I think I can figure out a simple puzzle box."

Shane shrugged. "If you say so."

"Shove it, Jethro."

"Name the place, *a ghrá*." He patted his stomach, just above his erection. "I'll shove it wherever you like."

"Pig."

His brows rose. "That's *Lord* Pig, thank you."

She huffed out a laugh. "Did you know your brother said almost the exact the same thing to Ruby once?"

"How did you...? No, never mind. Don't tell me." Her laughter was music to his ears. "Great minds and all that." He sat up, letting her get a good look at his morning wood. "Wanna go for a ride, little girl?" He waggled his brows, delighted when she laughed.

"Well—" Her cell phone rang, ending any hopes that he'd be getting his preferred breakfast. "Hello?"

Shane lay back on the bed with a sigh. "Tell Robin I said hi."

"Shane says hi."

He grinned ruefully. It looked like his dragon had to go back to work. He watched, fascinated, as her wings disappeared in a golden shower of sparks. Her skin turned creamy, her horns disappearing below her hair. When she turned around, her human Seeming rested on her skin, dazzling but mundane now that he'd seen what she *really* looked like.

He blew her a kiss and wrapped himself in his own Seeming, loving the moue of disappointment on her face. Apparently he wasn't the only one who liked the truth better than the fiction.

She hung up the phone and he realized he hadn't caught a word she'd said. "When do you go?"

"I have to meet with Etienne, Jaden and Robin in an hour." She shrugged. "Robin promised pastries if I made it in forty-five minutes."

"Damn." He stood and stretched, aware of her eyes drinking him in. He scratched his belly. "I'd ask for a good-bye kiss, but that might lead to you getting in trouble with your boss."

She shook her head. "I'd risk it."

Shane closed the distance between them and cupped her face. "Have a good day at work, *a ghrá.*" He poured all of his love into the kiss, hoping she felt even a fraction of what he did. He could work with fractions.

He'd always been good at math.

When he lifted his mouth from hers her eyes were dazed, her lips swollen. Her nipples poked his chest, begging for his touch. Instead, he stroked her cheek before pulling away. He couldn't interfere in her work. She'd never allow him to. They'd both wind up miserable, and the distraction could cause her death.

Besides, it was hot as hell knowing his mate could kick serious ass.

"Shower here. It'll be faster. I'll go back to the main house and grab you some clothes."

"And makeup."

He nodded, dragging on his jeans.

"And my shampoo and conditioner, because I'm not using anything in a man's shower."

His brows rose, but he pulled on his sweater anyway.

"And my soap."

"Anything else, Princess?"

"My brown boots with the gold buckles, my skinny jeans, underwear because I'm not going commando and my gold Michael Kors sweater. Oh, and my black overcoat, the one with all the pockets." She turned to the bathroom but turned back again almost immediately. "And I need the black box under my bed, and the—*eep!*"

He'd flung her naked over his shoulder. There was no way in hell he'd remember that list. A gold Michael Kors sweater? She had to be kidding him. "Might as well cart you back to the house rather than cart all that stuff here."

"I'm naked, Shane."

He opened the door to the outside, her shriek of outrage as the cold blasted her naked flesh making him laugh. "So I noticed."

She transformed in his arms to her full dragon form. Claws shredded the jeans covering his ass before she took off, pulling free as he instinctively covered his nakedness. "Asshole."

"I love you too!" He blew her a kiss before entering the studio once more. He hoped he had another pair of jeans, or his butt would be a frozen block before he got to the house.

Shane eyed the flying form of his mate as she landed on the roof of the house with a triumphant yell. Maybe he should have asked for a ride.

Jaden was too busy laughing his ass off to hear her low growls of warning. Robin merely looked amused, Etienne disturbed at the vampire's antics. "Goldschschläger," Jaden gasped. "Oh god, that's rich." Jaden wiped tears of mirth from his eyes before straightening up in his chair. His black eyes twinkled, an echo of Robin's eerie green flashing through them announcing their shared blood. "So. Were you well and truly fucked?"

Robin chuckled. Etienne looked pained.

Akane kept her expression deadpan. Toying with Jaden was fun, but only if he didn't catch on. "Shane did an adequate job."

Jaden's gaze roamed over her, but whatever he was looking for he didn't seem to find. "Remind me to have a little chat with him."

"Remind me to kill Tristan when I see him again." No one poisoned her with gold and got away with it.

"Any idea why he wanted us gone?" Etienne was frowning, ignoring the antics of Jaden, who'd picked up one of Duncan's pens and begun twirling it between his fingers. It appeared he'd taken a severe dislike to the vampire, much to Jaden's amusement.

They'd decided to hold this meeting at Jaden's home. Moira and Duncan had graciously agreed to stay out of the way, but Akane wouldn't be surprised if Jaden wasn't mentally keeping them in the loop. They'd agreed way too easily for it to be any other way.

"He probably believed the two of you would be an obstacle to completing his mission." Robin sat, one leg crossed over the other, and swung his foot lazily. He perched on the edge of Duncan's desk and watched them indulgently. He seemed highly amused by the fact that Etienne stayed as far as he could from Jaden. The Gray Court Sidhe had a reputation for avoiding the vampires of Oberon's court. Being forced into the position of working with one, and worse, one who held a higher rank than he did, had to be sticking in his upper-crust craw.

"If he really is Glorianna's agent it would be better to get him to work *with* us rather than against us." Jaden held up his hand to forestall Etienne's instant rejection of the idea. "Look, don't make me sing the Barney theme song. Moira hates it when I do that." He leaned back in his chair, balancing on two legs. "I know you don't love me, and I sure as hell don't love you, okay?" Jaden grinned at Robin. "We could always have Akane try again to seduce Tristan to the dark side."

"Won't work. He said any Sidhe could tell I'd been Claimed."

Jaden's chair hit the carpet. "Ow." He pushed up on his elbows, his brows in his hairline. "You mentioned sexual spelunking had happened. You left out the part about the fireworks. Hell, I wasn't sure Shane was *capable* of fireworks."

She shrugged and kept her voice even. "He took advantage of my weakened state." She blinked slowly. "As I said, he was adequate."

Jaden's lips twitched. "Welcome to the family." He leered at her. "You realize mating Shane puts you in my clan, under my rule, right?"

Shit. No, she hadn't thought of that. She wrinkled her nose and dropped the Vulcan act. "I want a divorce."

Robin threw his head back and laughed.

Etienne waved impatiently. "This is irrelevant. We have more important things to worry about than whose clan Akane belongs to."

Considering she'd avoided joining a clan like the plague, Akane felt it was *very* relevant. Thanks to who her mother was, Clan Blackthorn might now be perceived as having an advantage most other clans would kill to have: unlimited access to the Seer. But Etienne had a point. She could hash out the details with Jaden later.

Besides, if she absolutely had to belong to a clan, Clan Blackthorn was the one she'd pick anyway. "There has to be another way to get Tristan to work with us."

Jaden got up off the floor and righted his chair. "Maybe we can have Duncan talk to him? As former head of Clan Malmayne, he might be able to persuade him."

Akane bit her lip. "Unless he feels the same way toward Duncan and his bond with you that most of the White Court Sidhe feel."

Jaden growled. "Stuck-up, prickless bastards." His head tilted, his expression distant, His mates had to be speaking to him. A shy smile crossed his lips before he snapped back into the present. "He's willing, but he's not sure it will work."

Would she share the same kind of mental link with Shane? Was it a Sidhe thing or a vampire thing? Dragons didn't share that sort of mental bond, and Seers... Well, her mother said she'd always known her love would be brief, but the love the Seer held for her fallen mate couldn't be denied. Akane's father had been killed by a member of the Black Court a long time ago, leaving his mate and infant daughter to the tender mercies of the Courts. She stared into Jaden's eyes, that quirky little something that made them such good partners kicking in. "We could just break into his room—"

Jaden began to pace. "Have Red go through his computer files—"

"Sack the place—"

"Maybe even leave a little present for Henri." Jaden rubbed his hands together gleefully. "Daddy likey."

"It's too risky. If Henri or Tristan discover what you've done they could move on Ruby before we're ready, or worse, come up with a completely different plan."

"Tristan is Glorianna's agent, I'm almost positive of it."

Etienne glared at Akane. "I'm not." He turned to Robin. "I would suggest further investigation into Tristan's background. Perhaps there's something there that we can use against him or, even better, Henri."

Robin hopped off the table, light as a cat. "You do that." He turned to Jaden. "Are you ready to get back to work, Jaden?"

Jaden cracked his knuckles with an evil laugh.

Robin smiled serenely. "I'll take that as a yes." He turned to Akane. "You'll be working with Jaden on this from here on out." He patted her cheek, then Jaden's. "Make me proud, children."

With that Robin was gone in a swirl of wind and blowing papers.

"Shit." Jaden sighed, his hands on his hips. "Duncan's going to be pissed."

"Over being assigned this job?" Akane reached down and picked up one of the papers Robin had accidentally blown to the floor.

"Nope. He'll have to go through all that paperwork again." Jaden scratched his chin thoughtfully. "Oh wait. That was *my* paperwork. Guess my mate will have to lend me a hand since I have to work for the foreseeable future."

"Why does Robin place such trust in a vampire?" Etienne was glaring at them both.

Akane almost laughed in his face. "You weren't there when Clan Blackthorn was formed, were you?"

Etienne shook his head.

Jaden merely smiled, but that echo of Robin's green light flashed once more through his eyes, there and gone again.

"Jaden shares blood with Robin, confirmed by both Robin

and Oberon himself. Robin claims him as blood of his blood." Where was this animosity was coming from? Etienne was Gray Court; he should have gotten used to the vampires in the Court by now. "That means Robin Goodfellow considers Jaden family."

Etienne paled. "Ah." He stood and bowed. "I will get to work gathering the background information we need."

"Something that should have been done before you two even started. Seriously, Akane, where was your head? Up Shane's ass?"

She growled at Jaden. "Shut up. My primary objective was to protect Shane. My secondary objective was to fuck with Tristan Malmayne."

"You might want to discuss that last one with Shane. He might have an objection."

She let the star in the center of her eye grow, looking for Shane. His incandescent power danced across her senses, warming her. "Two completely different kinds of fucking." She grinned. "Trust me. I know the difference."

"Freaky dragon bitch."

Akane tilted her head. "Remind me some day to tell you how you got Robin's blood in you."

Jaden shuddered. "Please don't."

They barely acknowledged Etienne leaving the room. "You know?"

"I have...nightmares. Duncan tried to help me see what had happened, but when we were done he was... Gods, he was destroyed, and I still didn't know for certain what Robin did to me."

"Meaning Duncan turned around and re-blocked the memory." It was Akane's turn to shudder. "Jade, remember when you kidnapped Shane?"

"How could I forget? I still taste Kaitlynn occasionally when I burp. Blech."

Akane resisted rolling her eyes, barely. "Robin knew you'd taken Shane and, to get you to tell him where Shane was, he hurt you. When he realized you were trying to keep things together until Duncan got home he fixed you the only way he could."

Jaden nodded. "I kind of figured it was something like that." He ran his hand through his hair. "What bothers me is that Duncan is having a hard time letting it go. You and I, we know the risks of working for Robin. If he thinks we've betrayed him, we're toast."

"And you walked that fine line during Shane's abduction, praying you wouldn't cross it before it was too late."

Jaden nodded. "I love Duncan. Watching him suffer sucks. But this is one of the reasons I was worried they'd never accept me. I can't stop being a Blade, no matter how many times it hurts my bondmates. I can't let someone else get tortured or die just because Duncan and Moira might worry about me."

"I think they know that, Jade." She pointed toward the door, where Jaden's mates stood. Moira had her arms crossed over her chest, scowling at them both equally. Duncan had his arms around her waist, but his gaze was glued to Jaden's face.

"Oh goody. It's lecture time." Jaden dropped back into his chair and waved his mates into the room. "C'mon in, guys!" He started to tilt his chair back again.

Moira stopped him by dropping into his lap. "Idiot man."

Jaden pointed to himself. "Me?"

"Yes, you." Duncan's fingers buried themselves in Jaden's dark hair as he perched on the arm of Jaden's chair. "Of course we're going to worry, but we're not going to stop you from being a Blade. Just as we have to put up with your work, you'll have to learn to live with your family worrying about you."

Jaden's cheeks flushed. "I know that. But what happened with Robin could happen again."

Duncan shivered. "No. It won't." He pressed his fingers against Jaden's lips when the vampire started to protest. "Those were very special circumstances. You were trying to protect me in a strange sort of way. You were afraid killing Kaitlynn would make me hate you, so you played along, hoping I'd get here in time to save you all. Blame my father and Kaitlynn for that mess, not yourself. You kidnapped Shane on their orders, then kidnapped Ruby when you realized there wasn't anything else you could do to stop them short of revealing you were a Blade. If Kaitlynn or Cullen had figured it out they might have killed you before you could find out what was really going on in the clan."

"Killing Cullen and Kaitlynn without Robin or Oberon's consent could have resulted in Jaden not only being stripped of his Knighthood but also his life. So don't blame Robin either. Killing Kaitlynn on *your* orders, as head of his clan, was just fine." Akane shrugged when the trio's attention turned to her. "Besides, in a strange sort of way, if Robin hadn't done what he'd done Jaden might not have survived what West did to him." Another vampire had been working with Duncan's sister Kaitlynn to take Leo Dunne by force. He'd been promised Jaden's death in return for doing what Kaitlynn wanted. He might have succeeded if Robin hadn't already fed Jaden enough blood to change the vampire, making him stronger, faster and a lot less vulnerable.

The arrested expression on Duncan's face was priceless.

Moira frowned and tapped Jaden's chin. "I think Shane let Jaden take him."

Akane stared at Moira. "I think so too."

Jaden's hand flew into the air. "Ditto." He frowned, absently allowing his hand to be captured by Duncan. "But the question is, why?"

"It might have something to do with a vision he had." Once again, Akane had the trio's undivided attention. "What? You didn't know?"

Jaden started to laugh. He patted Moira's bottom with his free hand. "Gods, I love your family, sweetheart."

Moira rolled her eyes and got off Jaden's lap. "Shane's always been different, known things others didn't, but I've watched you. He doesn't show any of the signs you do when you're using your powers."

"His are completely different. I see the now. Shane sees the future."

Jaden jumped up, knocking Duncan to the floor. "Wait right here." He ran out of the room, only to return a few seconds later carrying a metal sculpture. Three figures entwined, two hovering protectively over one, encased in swirling green, gold and gray. He set the statue on Duncan's desk. "Do you know when he made this?"

"That's us, isn't it?" Moira touched the smallest figure. All of them were androgynous in their features, but something about the way that figure stood screamed female.

Duncan got up off the floor and dusted off his ass. "I'm inclined to believe so." He studied the figures, smiling slightly. "I know who the middle figure is, too."

Jaden rolled his eyes. "You, obviously."

Duncan snorted. "If believing that makes you sleep better at night, so be it."

Akane took the statue and tilted it up. "Look at the bottom."

Moira gasped. Jaden grinned, but his eyes looked a bit wild. Duncan merely nodded, as if he'd known what he'd see all along.

Shane had marked the date he'd created the statue on the bottom. It was dated precisely one year before Shane's abduction. "He made a similar one of Ruby and Leo."

"Has he made one of you?"

Akane avoided Duncan's knowing eyes. "There are two others he's made, and they scare even him." She described both the Robin figure and the one she assumed was Oberon, the one Shane hadn't been able to finish yet.

"Holy fuck." Jaden stared at the statue of the three mates. "Does he know what they mean?"

"I think he gets flashes, little glimpses, but until certain things happen they're mysteries to him. He must have known Moira was the female in this statue, but until he met you two he might not have known who you were."

"Damn. He has no idea who Robin's female is then, does he?"

Akane shook her head. It was obvious Jaden was thinking the same thing she was. "Or what's missing from Oberon's."

Jaden stood, suddenly every inch the Blade he was. "We need to find out."

"Before it's too late."

"Deal with the Malmaynes first." Duncan rubbed his hand down Jaden's back. "Robin's woman will show up. We just need to keep an eye out for her. We'll protect her so she doesn't fall."

Moira leaned back against the edge of Duncan's desk. "What about the vision of Oberon?"

"Shane says it's incomplete. He doesn't know yet what is supposed to be in the center of the sculpture."

Duncan wrapped his arms around his mates. "I think I do." He kissed each one on the cheek, his expression full of love for them. "Perhaps it's time for Oberon's heart to open up once more."

Akane stared at the three of them and decided Duncan might be right.

"Are you sure about this?" Shane watched Leo pace his office. He'd snuck out once he was sure Akane was gone. His brother was planning something, and Shane wanted in on it.

"As sure as I can be." Leo stopped and stared blankly at the wall. "Ruby and I have been over this again and again. Until I get the Malmaynes to realize they'll never have me this will just keep going on and on."

"The Energizer bunny of fuck-ups." Shane nodded. "Count me in."

Leo's smile was more of a grimace. "Thanks."

"Don't mention it. I mean that. If Akane finds out about this my ass is toast." Shane stood. "Where's Ruby?"

"Here." The little redhead swept into the room and curled up against her spouse. "Just finishing up some work before we face off with the Dork Brigade."

Shane grinned. "You've been hanging out with Jaden again."

She grinned back. "Nah. Robin's been by a few times." She tilted her head. "I think he's lonely."

Shane hid his shock. She'd seen below the surface Robin showed the world to find the desperately lonely fae beneath. "Yeah. I think so too."

"I think you're both insane, but okay." Leo jolted at the sound of the doorbell, betraying his nervousness. "Okay. It'll be okay."

"You want me to get the door?" Shane was already out of the office when his brother's soft consent reached his ears. Really, Leo wasn't made for this sort of fight. He was a wheeler, dealer and dreamer, running Fantasy Inc., a high-end party planning business used by corporations and politicians nationwide. Shane wasn't much better off, his artistic endeavors leaving little time to learn to fight. But he and Leo had the Blackthorns, Robin Goodfellow and Akane on their side.

They'd be just fine.

Shane opened Leo's front door to find Constance, Cecelia and Henri Malmayne on the other side. Cecelia was once again hanging all over Henri, while Constance had a coldly blank look on her face. "Hey, Leo!" He bellowed at the top of his lungs, making sure he sounded as rube as he could. "You've got Malmaynes at your door!"

"Let them in, Shane."

"Butlering for your brother now, Shane?" Cecelia sneered and sauntered past him. "Careful with my coat. It's Dior."

Shane took their coats, nodding back at Henri, who gave him a semi-civil nod and ignoring Constance the way she ignored him. "Leo's in the office, third door on the right."

The Malmaynes went past like a cold breeze. Shane scrunched their coats up into a ball and dropped them on the closet floor before joining his brother in the office.

The women had taken seats around Leo's desk, Henri standing behind Cecelia with one hand on her shoulder. Ruby was at Leo's right hand, the wedding ring she wore flashing as they clasped hands. Shane went to stand on his brother's left and let his visions flow over him.

He couldn't see what was about to happen; it was too close.

This was where Akane's talent was most useful, and he wished his dragoness were here by his side. He did his best, but the visions he was getting were about things that were coming.

And both Malmayne sisters were at the heart of it.

He listened with half an ear as Leo explained, yet again, that he and Ruby did not wish for a third in their marriage. The visions surrounding Cecelia Malmayne were...disturbing. Some were of what looked like torture. Others showed her having a relatively happy life with the man at her side. But in both cases a black pall hung over everything she did.

Constance, on the other hand, looked like she was sleeping with the devil. Who the hell was that in the vision? The man had horns and fangs, but Shane couldn't quite get a glimpse of his face. There was something familiar about him, about the way he moved, but no matter how hard Shane concentrated he couldn't get anything on him. If the man had been in the room Shane might have gotten a better read on him.

Should he warn her of the devil, or leave her to her fate?

"I'm telling you, Leo and I are fine the way things are. We don't want you here! The contract has been fulfilled. We know why you want a Child of Dunne and we're sick of dealing with this shit!" Ruby's rarely roused temper flared as she squared off with the Malmaynes, effectively dragging Shane back into the present. The vision of the devil man faded, and Shane decided to remain silent. Whatever Constance Malmayne was courting he had no doubt she deserved it. The aura surrounding her actions in his visions was black as pitch.

Constance stood. "There are ways to bear a child that don't involve sex, Ruby. If we could get Leo to donate his seed–"

"Fuck. You." Ruby pointed toward the door. "Out."

Leo stood. "We've given you the meeting you requested. You've heard my wife's response. The final answer is no. Have a nice life."

The Malmaynes stood. "You're going to regret this," Cecelia hissed on her way out. She ignored the way Henri tried to soothe her, clinging to her anger like a fiery cloak.

Constance shook her head. "We're sorry, Leo."

Shane's brows drew together. Oh, this sounded ominous. "Sorry for what?"

She just shook her head and left the office, closing the door quietly behind her.

"Shane."

"On it." Shane followed the Malmaynes out the door, just in time to hear Cecelia's outraged squawk. He grinned back at his brother. "I see they found their coats."

He watched them drive off and returned to his brother. "So. Thoughts?"

"They're fucking nuts."

"And dangerous." Ruby went to the chaise and lay down on it. "I swear, if it weren't for Duncan I'd vote the whole clan off the island."

Leo snorted and joined his wife on the chaise. Shane was amused to note it was built for one person, but Leo got around that by placing his small bondmate on top of him. "It never ends, Shane. Shit."

Shane shuddered. "It's almost over, Leo."

Leo frowned. "How do you know?"

He grimaced. "I know." He shivered and threw off the vision. "Listen, I have to get back. Akane's going to be there soon and she can't know I left the farm without back-up."

"Got it. Thanks, Shane."

"Anytime, bro."

Shane waved good-bye and managed to get back to the farm before Akane arrived. He was in his workshop when she came in, the cold air flowing in behind her in an arctic blast. "Hey, Akane."

"Can you read my mind?"

His hands paused on the metal he'd been slowly bending. "Pardon?"

"Can. You. Read. My. Mind?"

Shane stared at Akane and tried to ignore the slow way she'd drawled that, like he was unable to comprehend single-syllable words. His lips quirked as he realized why she was probably worried about something so trivial. "You want to know if I can read your mind."

Akane glared at him. "Don't make fun of me."

"I wouldn't dream of it." He tilted his head. "I'm not sure that's something I'm capable of." The relief on her face was grating. "But I'm willing to try if you are."

"Oh no. That's okay. I like my thoughts to stay in my own head."

He damn near chuckled at her badly hidden panic. "Still, it might come in handy if you're on an assignment and want to tell me you'll be late for dinner."

"Oh yeah. About that." Akane began backing toward the door of his studio. Her black trench coat was still on.

"Do I want to know where you're going?" Shane grabbed hold of the tie of her coat and pulled her in close, dropping a kiss on her nose.

"Probably not."

"Will Etienne be with you?" He resisted the urge to wrinkle his nose. The Sidhe Blade had been, at best, cool toward him. He didn't understand why, but if Etienne had plans concerning

Shane's mate he'd better think twice. Unlike his sister, Shane wasn't into sharing.

"Nope. Robin reassigned him. I'm working with Jaden again."

Shane picked her up and tossed her over his shoulder. He ignored her struggles and carted her back to the bedroom attached to his studio. "You know, if you're not careful I might drop you on your head. These floors are concrete."

"So?"

"So I hate repairing concrete." He tossed her on the bed. "Where are you going and how long do you think you'll be?"

"Why were you okay with this before I mentioned Jaden?"

"Because I've heard horror stories from Moira about how he operates. Spill."

She rolled her eyes. "We're breaking into the Malmayne estate and stealing Tristan's underwear."

"Oh, a fairy panty raid." He dropped on top of her, caging her in his arms. "I want you to *promise* you'll be careful."

She held up her hand. "I promise."

"Is Henri home?" He had no idea where the new head of the Malmayne clan had gone after the meeting with Leo.

Her star expanded as she looked for the man who'd plotted against Duncan. "Oh gods, yes. He's in bed with Cecelia, doing truly nasty things." She shuddered. "Sometimes I hate my talent."

"Do I want descriptions? Pictures? How-to manuals?" He laughed when she growled. "Where's Tristan?"

The star twitched. "He's currently in Henri's office, going through his files." She frowned. "He seems very excited by something."

"Then you'll just have to find out what that something is

and take it from him."

She blinked, the star shrinking down to its normal size. "In order to do that, you have to get off." She punched him in the stomach when he laughed again. "Not that way, you goob."

"Was that love tap supposed to hurt?" He rolled off her, still chuckling.

She growled and swiped at him, but he noticed her claws didn't really come close to him. "I hate you."

"I'd believe that if you hadn't been screaming my name last night." He helped her to her feet. "Come back here when you're done with work."

"Aileen will have hot chocolate waiting for me. What are you offering?"

He bent down and kissed her, telling her without words exactly what he was offering.

"Mmm." She licked her lips. "You'd better be awake when I get back."

He pulled her hips close to his body, letting his erection brush her stomach. Gods, she was so tiny compared to him. It amazed him how much strength was packed into that little package. "Maybe I'll have a thermos of hot chocolate waiting too."

She cupped his cheek. "I need you to do something for me while I work."

"Hmm?" He bent his head and kissed her palm, gratified to see the flush on her cheeks.

"Call my mother."

He immediately looked up.

"What?"

"Just checking. Yup, sky's still there."

"Look, Farm Boy, for once in your life, do what I asked without making smart-ass comments, okay? This is serious."

He bent once more and kissed her, but this time he kept it short and infinitely sweet. "As you wish."

She bit her lip. "We need to know two things, and only my mother can help." He nodded and waited for her to continue. "Who is the woman in Robin's statue, and who is missing from Oberon's."

"I can find out the one, but it's the other that's giving me fits."

She blinked. "Huh?"

He sighed. Sometimes explaining how his visions worked was more difficult than making the piece. Very few people seemed to understand that there were times when he just didn't understand what he was seeing. "Not all of the pieces are in place, or something else needs to happen before I can finish it, before it makes sense."

"Ah." She patted his chest. "In that case, perhaps that's the one you need to concentrate on."

He should have known the daughter of the Seer would understand. "I think Oberon's unfinished statue might have something to do with the whole child of Dunne thing." Akane was the only one he was willing to tell that to. Not even the Seer. It seemed wrong somehow. Every instinct he had told him that Oberon's unfinished statue was pivotal somehow. The missing piece *had* to have something to do with the prophecy. He just didn't know what. He wasn't even certain if it was a person, place or thing, and it was driving him insane.

"Should we warn the rest of your family?"

"Only if Jaden promises to keep quiet. This...there's something about that statue that tells me too many people who know could seriously screw things up."

"Robin will *have* to know, but if we keep it to only him, would that be all right?"

Shane nodded reluctantly. "I trust Robin."

"Thank you."

Shane was getting tired of the Hob popping in and out as he damn well pleased. "Can't you knock or something?"

A knocking sound drummed through the building, but Shane couldn't tell where it was coming from.

"Smart ass."

Robin's blue eyes appeared before the Hob did, much like the Cheshire Cat's grin. He bowed once he was fully in the room. "I try my best."

Shane couldn't stop himself. Robin just made him smile. "You heard us?"

"Yes." He stared through the wall, and damn if he wasn't looking right where Oberon's statue was sitting, even though it was on the other side. "I will keep silent on your vision of Oberon's future until I am forced to speak of it."

"Thank you." Relief washed through him. One of the possible blocks to Oberon's future had been removed. The Hob *always* kept his word. "Once I see more I promise I'll tell you, but it's still very murky." He shook his head. "I just know a Dunne has a hand in it."

"Could it be one of your future nieces or nephews will fulfill the prophecy?"

"A child of Dunne will change the world as we know it." Robin began to fade from view. "I'm beginning to agree more and more with Jaden. Be careful, children. More is at stake than you could possibly understand." The Hob disappeared, but Shane was certain he'd soon reappear again.

"What does Jaden think?" Shane cradled Akane close,

hoping to delay her departure a little bit. He'd missed her badly during the day.

"That the Child is either you, Leo or Moira."

Shane nodded. He'd already known that. "I think he's right."

Chapter Six

Shane waited until Jaden and Akane left the farm before pulling out his cell. He had a few things to discuss with Akane's mother outside of the vision he'd had of Robin. He dialed the Seer's number and listened to it ring.

"Hello, Shane."

He smiled. Even before Caller ID she'd always known who was calling. "Hello. I need your help with a vision and with the Malmayne situation."

"You know what I have to do."

He grimaced. He hated this part. "Yes. I consent."

Shane gasped as the Seer invaded his mind, read his visions. Because he was also to some extent a Seer, the only way for her to get an accurate read on the questions he had was to take a look at his visions, to know what drove his hands to create. All the possibilities floated in his mind, but his hands only created the most likely outcome. The closer the event, the more accurate the vision until he was moved to go to his studio and bend metal and glass. The mental rifling she did through his mind hurt like hell as she basically took his gift and used it as her own.

He was pale and sweating when she was done, his head pounding and his heart racing. All he wanted in that moment was to curl up on the bed around his mate, but that comfort was denied him. Shane tried to shake off the effects, but only time would erase them. "What do you think?"

"I think that soon the second piece will be complete."

Shit. That meant the event the child of Dunne was supposed to influence was closer than his visions had led him to believe. "And Robin's?"

"The Hob will find his heart before the Gray King does. Something must be lost in order to be found again. The damage that was done to the King's soul will finally be healed."

"Vague as always." He could almost picture her smile. "And the Malmaynes?" The vision he'd had in Leo's office came back to him in all its gory detail. If things went the way he'd seen, Shane would be in a world of hurt.

"Ruby is safe. It is *your* back you must watch."

A jolt of fear shot down his spine, chilling him. He'd been right. He'd become a target again. Shit. "What would they want with me?"

"They know. Tell my daughter I said be careful."

She hung up before he could ask what she meant. The possible threat to Akane scared him more than any real threat to himself. He grabbed his coat and his car keys and headed out of the studio, his only thought to be with his fiancée.

Akane watched through her inner sight as Jaden misted through the keyhole of the Malmayne's front door. No one could perform a B&E like a vampire. Akane's role was that of lookout, something she was infinitely suited for. She sat on the hood of her car, her senses wide open, following Jaden mentally through a house he was all too familiar with. She'd almost forgotten he'd broken into the Malmayne mansion twice before, once to collect information on Charles Malmayne, Duncan's uncle, and once to exact justice on Charles for working with the Black. They'd gotten to the estate in fifteen minutes, Jaden driving like a bat out of hell in order to do it. Akane still wasn't sure their wheels had been on the ground at any given time, but Jaden said he'd done this before and she believed him.

Jaden whisked through the house, sometimes mist, sometimes a silent predator. Already Akane was seeing signs the Malmaynes were on the downward spiral to the Black. The estate seemed surrounded by a dark miasma. Sometimes she wished she had Shane's talent for seeing the future. She wasn't sure anymore how many of the Malmaynes could be saved.

Jaden found Tristan still going through Henri's things. He quickly subdued the White Court Sidhe, not giving him time to protest or even realize a vampire had snuck up on him. Akane couldn't blame him. White Court Sidhe were notorious for attacking vampires on sight, not caring if they were Gray Court or Black. Tristan might know who Jaden was on an intellectual level, but she wasn't willing to bet Jaden's life on whether or not Tristan would react instinctively and try to kill Jaden.

Jaden trussed up Tristan like a roped calf, arms and legs together. He then turned his attention to whatever had caught Tristan's and grinned. "I'm calling Red." He spoke out loud, knowing Akane would be able to hear him even if he couldn't hear her. They'd never formed even a light blood bond; the vampire had shied away from the thought from the very beginning of their partnership five years ago. She'd never known if his bond with Duncan had anything to do with that, or the fact that she was a dragon and he didn't know if she'd give him indigestion.

Knowing Jaden, the answer could be both.

"Okay. Red's going through the files." Robin's pet Gremlin was a wizard at anything electronic, but he specialized in hacking and data retrieval. He'd managed to pull data off of drives that had been completely reformatted, something the humans still hadn't figured out how to do. "He says this time Henri must have known we'd get a Gremlin in on the action because the computer is slightly better protected than last time." He sat in Henri's chair and put his feet up on the unconscious Sidhe. "In other words, the computer's legs are halfway closed instead of wide open."

Akane snorted, amused. The running commentary was entertaining, but she'd rather be back in Shane's nice warm studio.

"Got it. And according to Red, Henri is just taking Charles's plan and upping it a notch or two."

"Wonderful." Jaden might not be able to hear or see Akane, but she couldn't stop herself from replying anyway. Charles had wanted both Moira and Jaden tossed to Duncan's curb and Leo mated to either Cecelia or Constance, his daughters. The Malmayne's blindness where it came to Sean Dunne's children and the possibility one of them would fulfill the prophecy would have tickled her if she didn't understand the dangers. More than one person over the years had heard her mother's words but had refused to *listen*. It never ended well for the willfully blind.

"On my way back. Warm up the car for me, will ya? It's cold enough out here to freeze off the Black Queen's tits." He hefted the trussed up Tristan on his shoulder. "Oh, and I'm bringing you a present. You can thank me later."

"I'd prefer chocolates." She'd have to figure out a way to get Tristan to work with them. If she didn't, she'd have no choice but to take him out of the game and pray there were no other White Court agents running around on her case. Hopefully Tristan had lied about having a partner or their goose could be cooked.

She withdrew her vision as soon as Jaden passed the Malmayne perimeter and began sprinting up the road toward her. She stretched, her ass half frozen from sitting on the hood of her car for so long.

"So? How'd it go?"

Akane shrieked and fell off the hood.

"Sorry."

She would have believed Shane if he hadn't been laughing so hard.

"What the fuck are you doing here, Jethro?" Smoke poured out of her nose, her annoyance at an all-time high.

"I missed you." He held out his hand and pulled her to her feet. "You sure looked cold there, Miz Akane."

She *knew* he did it just to annoy the fuck out of her. It was the only explanation as to why he did that hick drawl thing, because Shane's voice was normally smooth as silk and warmer than fur.

"Hey, Shane." Jaden jogged up to them, Tristan bouncing on his shoulder like a sack of potatoes. "Take this, will you?" He flung the unconscious Sidhe at Shane, who caught him with a surprised grunt. "Red called. He thinks Henri is planning on moving on Ruby sometime in the next few days. We need to step up the security around both Ruby and Leo."

Akane tilted her head like she was actually thinking about it. "What's a step above Robin Goodfellow?"

Jaden opened his mouth, but he wisely shut it again. He turned his attention instead to Shane. "Had any visions lately?"

Shane shook his head and shoved Tristan in the back of his Corvette. He wasn't exactly gentle about it either. "I can't make the visions come to me. They show up when they show up."

Shane was hiding something from her. His expression was closed, but the glimpse of fear she'd seen before he'd turned away from them told her more than words could.

Shane was never afraid, but today he was.

"Think the Seer might be able to help you with that?"

Shane stared at Jaden. "There's always a price to pay when you consult the Seer."

Akane bit her lip. "What payment have you made?" When Shane didn't answer, she paled. "Shane? Tell me I'm not part of the payment."

He glared at her. "You're kidding me, right? You think even your mother could make me Claim you if fate hadn't made you mine?"

Her cheeks flushed. "It was a thought." She shook her finger in his face. "But you *are* going to tell me what price she's made you pay."

He nodded. "But not now."

"This is all very touching, but McAsshole is starting to wake up." Jaden leaned in the door of the Corvette. "Hello, Sleeping Beauty." He reared back and tsk'd as Tristan kicked out at him, tumbling himself to the floor in the process as his feet were still tied to his wrists. "Now don't you feel stupid? Guess who gets to sit on the corner stool after class?"

Akane rolled her eyes. "Way to make friends and influence people, Jade."

"I try." The vampire put his hand to his chest dramatically. "Why don't we take him back to the Dunne farm and introduce him to Sean?"

The wicked gleam in Shane's eyes did not bode well for the Sidhe. "I like that plan." He got into the driver's seat before

Akane could say a word. "Meet you there."

"Moira and Duncan will be there shortly." Jaden got in the driver's seat of her Boxster. "Call Leo. They should be there too. Maybe if all the Dunnes talk to Tristan he'll be more easily persuaded to help."

"Fine." She got in and let Jaden drive her baby once more and called Leo.

He picked up on the first ring. "Hello?"

"We need you and Ruby to head for your parents' farm." She explained their plan to Leo, who readily agreed. "Meet you there."

Akane smiled as they pulled onto Sean's land. It seriously sucked, but damn if this wasn't becoming home.

Shane pulled the wriggling Sidhe out of the back of his car. "Hush. You don't want to piss off my father, do you?"

Tristan stopped wriggling. "You kill me and Glorianna will come down on you like the wrath of god."

Shane untied the Sidhe's feet and set him down. "You honestly believe that?" When Tristan nodded, Shane whistled.

The Sidhe's eyes widened as fifty pounds of salamander landed in front of Shane, his fiery tail going a mile a minute. Happy flames danced up and down the salamander's sides and legs. "Down, boy."

Sal toned down his inner fire, his Seeming covering his scales until a German Shepherd sat at his feet.

Shane pointed to Tristan. "Guard."

Sal's gaze locked on Tristan. His tail stopped wagging as the salamander went to work, obeying Shane's command the way he'd obey Akane's. The salamander was smarter than most gave it credit for. It had known from the beginning that Akane belonged to Shane and had treated him accordingly.

Shane turned to the front of the house, ready to let his parents know what was about to happen, but he needn't have bothered. Sean Dunne stood on the top step, his hands in the pockets of his thick jacket, his expression hard as he stared at Tristan. "Give me one good reason why someone should be able to find your body after today."

Tristan glared up at the leprechaun. "Glorianna will kill you."

Sean smiled, and Shane took a step toward him. "Da. We need him."

"He hurt my daughter-in-law." Sean had adored Akane from the very beginning. Tristan wasn't going to be forgiven easily, not by the leprechaun.

"I thought it would knock her unconscious, not send her into heat."

"And you think that's an adequate excuse? You effectively fed her a date-rape drug."

Tristan winced. "I'm sorry."

From the way the ground rumbled under their feet Sean was far from appeased. "What if the gold had been poison to her? She's a hybrid. It could have killed her." His father's voice was rich with the lilt of Ireland and filled with anger. "What would you have told me then when my son pined away from mate sickness? When my wife broke from grief? Would you have told me 'oops'?" Shane watched as his father descended the steps to stand before Tristan, one hand resting easily on the top of Sal's head. Jaden pulled up behind the Corvette and got slowly out of Akane's car, his gaze firmly on Sean.

Akane hopped out and raced over to Shane. "Your brother-in-law drives like a freaking maniac." She stopped in front of Sean and stood on her tip-toes to press a kiss to his cheek.

"Aileen have any hot chocolate going? I'm freezing."

Sean spared her a soft smile. "Go on in, Akane. I'm sure Aileen will be more than happy to make you some."

"Sweet." She started off up the stairs. Without pausing she yelled back, "Don't kill him, Sean." She glanced back over her shoulder and tossed Shane's father a wicked grin. "I have *plans* for him." She sauntered into the house, the sound of the screen door slamming shut loud in the cold air.

Sean stepped back from Tristan. "One step wrong and you'll be dead before you know what happened to you." He shot Tristan one last glare before following Akane into the house without a backward glance.

"I love that man." Jaden sniffed and wiped away an imaginary tear.

Shane nodded. "He's the best." He'd have to tell his father about his chat with the Seer. If what he suspected was right, Akane was in serious danger.

Jaden took hold of Tristan's arm. "Call off Sal. I'll escort our guest inside."

"Sal. Heel." Sal trotted to sit beside Shane, his tail once more going a mile a minute. Just as he got to the front door Leo and Ruby pulled up in their Land Rover. Behind the wheel was, of all people, the Hob. Somehow, Shane wasn't surprised. "C'mon in. I think Ma's making hot chocolate."

The Hob lifted Ruby out of the SUV, much to her husband's obvious annoyance. Leo had been just a hair slower than Robin. "Hey, Shane!" Ruby waved, nearly knocking the Hob over. "Sorry, Robin."

Robin shook his head and placed her on the ground. "You are a dangerous woman, Ruby Halloway Dunne."

She reached up and patted his cheek. "And don't you forget

it." She took hold of her husband's arm and walked with him to the house. The grin on Leo's face was wicked. He was getting used to Ruby's ways and must have finally figured out Robin wouldn't hurt a hair on her head.

The Hob, however, looked delightedly shocked. Shane paused, wondering that such a simple gesture put such a look of yearning on Robin's face before it was hastily wiped away. "So." Robin cleared his throat and sauntered to the house. Again, he was dressed way too lightly for the weather. A simple black coat with silver buttons reached his knees, but it was in no way thick enough to keep the cold air from reaching his skin. Black jeans were tucked into high black boots. Shane would bet anything another silk shirt lay under that jacket. Perched on his head was a black cowboy hat with a silver band. His red hair blew about in the cold air, unconfined by anything except that hat. "You have Tristan. What do you plan on doing with him?"

"If my father has his way, feed him to the cat."

"That hardly seems like a fitting punishment for hurting your fiancée."

"You haven't seen the cat."

Robin hopped up the steps and quickly entered the house, but not before rolling his eyes. "Come along, Shane."

"Yes, sir." He patted Sal one last time on the head and set the salamander to guarding the house. He didn't want another surprise attack from the Malmaynes during a family meeting. The last one had blown up Akane's car and lost them the barn, but gained them Sal.

This time they might not be so lucky.

He stepped into the house and headed for the kitchen, the heart of his parents' home. He accepted the hot chocolate his mother handed him and settled in next to Akane who, for the first time, did not growl or glare at him. She put her head against his shoulder wearily, like it was the most natural thing in the world, and not something that stopped the conversation dead in its tracks.

"What?" Akane yawned. "I'm tired."

Moira relaxed. He hadn't even realized how tense his sister was around his bondmate until that moment. "We have to figure out the best way to protect Leo and Ruby."

Robin coughed.

"When Robin is busy elsewhere."

Everyone chuckled, even Robin.

Shane took a deep breath. "I have a message from the Seer."

Akane lifted her head. "What did my mother say?"

"First, she said to tell you hello."

Akane nodded impatiently. "And?"

"'Ruby is safe. It is *your* back you must watch.'"

"Mine?" Akane pointed to herself.

Shane shook his head. "No. Mine."

"What?" Akane jumped out of her seat, flames dancing in her eyes. Her golden horns appeared on her head.

"She also said they know and to tell you to be careful."

Akane stilled. "They know what?"

"I'm not sure. That you broke into their house?"

"That Shane has visions?" Robin examined his fingernails. "If they have such a gift in their hands they might be able to interpret, or even interrupt, prophecy."

Aileen's fist clenched on the table. "They are not taking my child from me again." Golden sparks danced across her skin as the full-blood Sidhe's fear took over.

"We'll protect him, Ma." Moira gestured to her mates. "Jaden can watch over him when Akane's asleep."

Jaden nodded. "It won't be a problem."

Leo sighed. "I feel kind of useless. I'm surrounded by Blades. Sit. Stay. Good boy. Woof."

"You're still their primary target. Don't forget that." Akane patted his shoulder. "If they can get you to agree to a mating they think they've succeeded. If Shane has become a target it's because they know about the visions."

"Which means they're willing to hurt him where they aren't willing to hurt Leo." Sean sighed. "We need this over with. I'm tired of my family being in danger."

Tristan watched everything silently. Shane had no idea what was going through the Sidhe's head. Tristan's expression was carefully closed off, giving no clue to what he was thinking.

Ruby bit her lip. "If we stay on our land, Leo should be able to keep us both safe, right? He's bonded there the way Sean is here. He could use the land itself to stop someone."

"Only if he knows they're coming," Akane pointed out.

Ruby snorted. "Please. The day something gets past Robin Goodfellow is the day I go up on the roof naked and sing show tunes."

Everyone turned and stared at the small human perched delicately on her husband's lap. "Ruby," Leo sighed. His hand covered his eyes. "Don't tempt him."

Robin tilted his head, his expression thoughtful. He tapped one black fingernail against his chin. "Would it be worth it?"

Ruby patted her husband's cheek. "It's okay. I trust him."

That simple, honest answer brought a flush to the Hob's cheeks. Shane was certain that the number of times the Hob had blushed could be counted on one hand.

But then the Hob's attention turned to Tristan and any trace of a blush was gone. He straddled the man's chair, those black nails lengthening into talons. His blue eyes flashed to glowing green. Tristan paled beneath the cold touch of the Hob's claws.

"You are at the heart of this."

Tristan swallowed so hard his Adam's apple bobbed visibly. "I am an agent of the White Queen."

"You are interfering in a duly appointed Blade's operation." One claw drifted down Tristan's cheek, leaving behind a thin trail of blood. His hand gripped Tristan's chin tightly. "Now. Don't lie to me. I will know it if you lie."

Jaden began to pant and clutch his stomach. He moaned, the sound agonized.

"Shit." Duncan stood and hauled Jaden to his feet. "Moira, I need you."

The two concentrated on Jaden and, whatever they did, it soothed the vampire. He slumped between them, the two holding him, protecting him from whatever it was that tormented him.

"Get him out or the memories will break free." Robin turned his head. "Patrol if you must, or slip away and help him forget, but for now he must be removed."

Duncan nodded distantly, but not for one moment did Shane think he was angry with the Hob. The Sidhe was building a fantasy for his mate, keeping Jaden trapped there to protect him from whatever painful memories were trying to erupt.

The trio walked slowly out of the room, headed for the stairs. Duncan and Moira had decided to distract their mate, and Shane just hoped they didn't get too loud. There were just some things a man shouldn't hear his baby sister doing.

"So much for Duncan talking to Tristan." Akane flopped back down next to Shane and stared at the Sidhe currently serving as Robin's perch. "Are you beginning to understand what's really going on?"

"Why are they protecting a vampire?" Tristan shook his head and earned himself another scratch from Robin's claws. "He's a vile child of the Dark Queen. I will *never* understand how they can just accept him that way."

Akane gasped when Shane began to laugh. "You will. Oh, you will understand, and when you do you'll regret those words."

Akane opened her inner sight and gasped. Shane's power rippled around him, his visions in overdrive. "Something tells me Tristan is going to become a Shane Joloun original."

"Soon. Not yet. Other things must happen first before his future comes to pass."

"Let him see." Robin crooned the words as he tapped Tristan's forehead. "Let him see what he risks by his refusal to help us."

Shane stood. "I'm not sure. I've never dropped my Seeming around anyone but my family before."

Robin nodded without ever taking his eyes off of Tristan. "Trust me, Shane."

Shane sighed and dropped his Seeming. Ruby gasped as Shane's true appearance dazzled everyone in the room. He was a golden god, and Akane ached to lick him one inch at a time. His power swirled around him, pieces of art being created in light, and Akane longed to touch, to hold. To hoard. He pushed his longer hair behind his ears, and for the first time she noticed the delicate points. Looking even closer she realized he had the classic oval pupils of the Sidhe.

"Wow," Ruby breathed.

Tristan blinked. "Gods above. He's a true hybrid." His breath hitched. "I'd heard tales, but I assumed they were wrong, that Shane was merely a closer blend than most between his parents. But no. He's truly a hybrid."

Robin nodded. "Rarest of the rare, and mated to another true hybrid as well."

Tristan's eyes closed. "Akane."

"You didn't believe the daughter of the Seer was also a hybrid?" Robin's laugh was low. "More fool you."

Tristan's eyes opened. He stared at Akane, who'd also dropped her Seeming. While she didn't have Shane's golden splendor, her own looks were intimidating in their own way. She hissed at Tristan but left her wings furled. The kitchen was too small to stretch them out. That night in the park he hadn't gotten a good look at her. Now he could see her in all her glory, and he winced at the sight.

"Double wow." A feather-light touch along her wings startled her. "That is *so* cool." She turned to find Ruby practically bouncing around her like an over-eager Tigger while Leo looked on indulgently. Ruby played with her claws briefly and eyed her horns before she looked over at Shane. "You have *got* to use her as a model."

Shane smiled at his bubbly sister-in-law and wrapped his arms around Akane, careful of her wings. She maneuvered them so that he could rest his head against her shoulder. "I already did."

"Good." Ruby turned to Robin. "You know, I'm tired of this song and dance where the Malmaynes try and take me to force Leo to be a sperm donor. Can we change the music?"

Robin blinked. "Ah." His face stilled, but Shane could almost see the plans whirling through the Hob's head at lightning speed. "What an excellent suggestion." He tapped his claw on Tristan's chin much the same way he tapped it on his own. "We know Charles and Cullen were working with the Black. Do we yet have proof that Henri is as well?"

"Even if we do, if we execute him someone else will just take his place." Sean was practically growling, his own Seeming failing. Brown swirls appeared on his suddenly darker skin, his eyes turning a stormy blue-green. "Cecelia or Constance will see to it that another male of the blood becomes lord of the clan."

"So, 'tis a hydra, not a snake, we play with here." Robin stood and got a fresh mug of hot chocolate. He handed it to Ruby, who smiled and accepted it with quiet thanks. "The only way to stop a hydra is to lop off its heads and burn the stumps."

Leo's eyes were wide, his expression horrified. "You're talking about the death of a clan."

Tristan twitched. "My clan is not Black."

"But they are no longer entirely White, either." Robin paused and waved his hand. Tristan's bindings fell, tattered, to the ground. "Henri, Cecelia and Constance are but a part of the whole."

"Just because my clan objected to Duncan's mating a vampire does not mean all of them are turning to the Black." Tristan stood and faced the Hob squarely, but Shane could see the fear in him.

"But they follow where their leaders take them, even if it's into darkness." The Hob sighed and held up his hand as Tristan began to protest. "No. There is a haven for those who do not wish to fall, but not all will take it and you know it."

"The Gray Court." Tristan said it without emotion, but his shoulders slumped.

"Aye." Robin smiled. "'Tis not a bad place to wash ashore

when you are set adrift."

"And all those who do will be clanless."

"Better clanless than a bad guy." Ruby sipped her hot chocolate. "Think about it. Would you rather work for Robin or against him?" She shrugged. "I know which team *I'd* bat for."

"You wouldn't be clanless for long," Duncan added, stepping into the room. He looked weary, but relieved. Whatever he and Moira had done for Jaden must have worked. "If you object to Clan Blackthorn, there are other Gray Clans who would accept you and any who followed you."

"You bested a dragon and a seer. If you wish, training as a Blade would be made available to you."

Tristan ran his fingers through his hair. "We haven't fallen to the Black."

"Are you sure?" Shane held out his hands, his light dancing around him, forming odd shapes. "Want to see what the future holds?"

"Yes." There was no hesitation in Tristan's voice.

"Then watch." Shane exhaled, and his lights danced.

When he was done Tristan was pale and sweating. Akane didn't understand half of the images in Shane's lights but apparently Tristan did. "Dear gods. What have they done?" He collapsed into his chair, his head in his hands. "What have *we* done?"

"What's that supposed to mean?" Leo was watching the whole thing. Gods alone knew what was going on behind those green eyes of his, but Akane doubted it was the same thing going through hers. Leo was a good man, but he wasn't a Blade and never would be.

"You helped, didn't you?" Akane opened her sight, hoping she'd catch a glimpse of how Tristan wound up Glorianna's errand boy on this one. "She knew all along, didn't she?"

"Who?" Leo threw his hands up. "I swear if someone doesn't start explaining this shit to me I'm going to explode!" Golden sparks danced across his skin and through his hair.

"Then let me shed some light for you." Akane allowed her inner fire to glow under her skin, reminding Tristan just what he was dealing with. "You helped first Cullen, then Kaitlynn, and finally Charles, didn't you?"

Tristan nodded. "My goal was to get information, but somehow each one died before I had enough to bring to Glorianna. She blames Jaden rather than my own failures." He lifted his head, his face ravaged. "If they succeed... But how do I take visions to my Queen as proof?"

"You don't. Jaden said you found enough on Henri's computer to get him eliminated."

"But the hydra would live on." Robin, almost forgotten he'd gone so still and quiet, stepped into Akane's light. "We need to chop off *all* the heads."

"Or fulfill the prophecy." Shane slipped his arms around Akane, unafraid of her fire. "One way or another, we have to stop Henri from gaining control of Leo."

"The thing is, the prophecy is so fucking vague how will we even know if it's been fulfilled?"

"What *is* the prophecy?" Tristan stared around at all of them, his confusion clear. "I've heard that we need the child of Dunne but I'm not far enough in the inner circle to find out anything more."

Akane spoke the words her mother had given Clan Malmayne, sealing all of their fates. "The child of Dunne will one day perform an act that will change our world."

Tristan blinked. "That's it?"

Akane shrugged. "That's it."

"But...that could be any of you!"

"Exactly. But for some reason the Malmaynes have it in their thick skulls that only Leo can produce the child spoken of in the prophecy."

Tristan shook his head. "But...what about Sean's children? I'd think one of them would be the one to fulfill the prophecy, not some unnamed, unborn child." His expression turned horrified. "Unless that was why they're pushing so hard for marriage with Leo. They're hedging their bets."

"That's what we think." Duncan pushed away from the wall and stared up at the ceiling. "Jaden's out. Moira's going to stay with him a bit longer and make sure the nightmares don't return." He transferred his gaze to Tristan, silver lights dancing around him like fireflies, a Sidhe lord in full wrath. Tristan's power paled beside Duncan's. "Now. Tell me what the hell is going on in my former clan."

He left unspoken the *or else.*

Chapter Seven

"I've been meaning to ask you something."

Akane glanced up at Shane through her lashes. They'd retired to Shane's workshop, and now he was at his workbench, staring into space. He was busy curling metal shavings, for what she had no clue. "About?"

"The tattoo on my arm."

Akane froze. Tattoo? "Let me see." She grabbed hold of his arm and pulled it toward her. There, curled on his forearm, was her dragon, its tail forming the symbol of infinity. She thought back to when they'd made love, and her idea that, if he was going to mate a dragon, he was going to do it right. She barely remembered taking the energy of their combined orgasm and focusing it on his arm. It had been pure instinct to do so, and now they were bound by more than a Sidhe's Claiming. "Oh crap."

"What?"

"Crappity crap crap." She ran her fingers through her hair. What was she supposed to do now? This wasn't supposed to happen yet!

A slow grin began to take over Shane's face. "You marked me."

Akane began to back up as Shane started toward her, a

feral gleam in his eye. "You know, maybe we should concentrate on what Tristan said earlier."

"About what? Henri, the computer files, or his refusal to name his partner?"

Akane nodded.

"Nah. I'm more interested in my new tat, Miz Akane." He stroked his finger down the dragon's back, and Akane shivered. Beneath her skin she could feel her wings trying to unfurl.

They were back in his studio, the one place where Shane was completely free to be himself. Akane found herself liking the space more and more the longer she stayed here, but if they were going to live on the damn farm she planned on having her own house built. She'd have to corner Sean and find out what piece of land he was willing to let his son and daughter-in-law have. Hell, she planned on making Shane buy her a condo in Omaha. She already owned one in New York and L.A.

Maybe she could get him to buy one in Milan?

"Eep!" She dodged out of the way of his grasping hands, startled to realize how close she'd allowed him to get to her. All because she'd been distracted by visions of enjoying her mate in Italy. Pasta and piazzas and her mate naked in the light of Milan? Or better yet, Tuscany? Mrow. "Down boy."

"You mated me." The gleam in his eye did not bode well for her plans that evening. She was tired, but Robin had requested she do an aerial recon over Leo's place "just in case". When the Hob asked you to do something "just in case" it usually meant he had a good idea that something was about to go down and you were his best defense against it.

Shane ran his finger down the front of the dragon, and Akane squealed. It was like he'd stroked her from head to toe. She shook her finger at him. "Bad Shane!"

His brows rose. "Oh?" That wicked, evil finger flicked over

the horns of his dragon tattoo and Akane's knees damn near gave out. She stumbled back against his workbench, her pussy clenching at the sensations he'd managed to pull from her just by touching her mark on his arm.

"Interesting."

"Shane." He looked way too satisfied, and she had far too much to do to get sucked in right then. Robin was waiting for... Oh. *Oh.* Her head fell back as his fingers continued to stroke his tattoo in all the right places. "Oh fuck. Shane."

"What a good idea." Shane grabbed her shoulders and pushed her to her knees. "Mind giving me a hand with something?"

Akane rolled her eyes. "Let me guess."

He pulled down his zipper and unleashed the beast. "Good guess." His finger stroked between the dragon's thighs and Akane jumped. "But I have a unique rewards system set up by my loving fiancée."

Akane smirked. "Does she know you're about to do me in your workroom?"

Shane's expression was anything but innocent. "Shh. Don't tell her."

Akane snorted and licked the head of his cock. She looked up from under her lashes, using every wile she'd ever used on a mark to get Shane to be as crazy for her as she was for him. "If she finds out she'll fry your ass."

"Then we'd better make this quick. She'll be back any minute now."

Akane blew warm smoke over his cock. "Is she dangerous?"

Shane nodded. He couldn't seem to take his eyes off the sight of her lips so close to his cock. Akane licked them, and those sapphire eyes darkened with want. "More dangerous than you could ever imagine."

She smiled. She liked that. She rewarded him by taking him into her mouth, sucking on the head of his cock until his hand left that damn tattoo. He buried his hands in her hair, toying with the long curls. He let her set the pace, how deep she took him. But those hands remained, reminding her that of what she needed. All she had to do was drop enough of her Seeming to allow her horns to peek through, and Shane would take care of her.

If she let him, he would always take care of her.

Shane watched as Akane swallowed him down. He bit back a moan at the feel of her hot mouth around his dick. Gods, he'd never get enough of the heat of his dragon mate. It took everything in him not to thrust, not to force himself further into her mouth. He wanted her to do this, to know that he might be able to torture her with the tattoo but all she had to do was give him one look from those pretty eyes of hers and he was lost.

She glanced up at him and suckled, her tongue stroking the underside of his cock in a firm, mind-blowing rhythm. Shane swore his eyes crossed. "Gods, *a ghrà*. Suck it. Please."

Akane obeyed, her head bobbing, her curls swinging around her face. He bent down and managed to reach her nipple. He stroked it, teased it, twisted it until her hips were moving, practically begging him to take down her jeans and fuck her.

"I'm going to fuck you on my workbench. I'm going to lift you up, rip those jeans off and spread you wide." Shane couldn't stop himself. He began to fuck her mouth, sliding between her lips. He glared wildly at the table top, the metal shavings he'd been toying with still there. He couldn't put her naked ass onto the table without damaging it, not with the metal there.

"It won't hurt me, remember?"

He stared at her, confused. What in hell was she talking about?

Akane rolled her eyes and stood. "Someone's brains have traveled south." She breathed flame hot enough to melt metal, smiling in satisfaction as it pooled down to molten silver and copper. "There. Problem solved."

He nodded. "I love an inventive woman."

He unzipped her jeans. Oh. Oh hell, she'd worn white lace again. He was such a goner. He tugged the jeans down her legs, loving the smooth, silky skin he unveiled. Shane gripped her hips and pulled her close, licking that white lace and what lay beneath.

She tapped the top of his head. "Up on the table, Farm Boy."

That wicked smile was back on her face. He had no idea what she had in mind, but if the heat in her gaze was any indication he was going to love every minute of it. Shane slipped his pants and shoes off before hopping onto the table. Strangely, the heat from the silver didn't seem to bother him. Perhaps the mark she'd given him protected him?

Akane didn't seem to notice anything out of the ordinary. She slid her top and jeans off, revealing more white lace.

Shane stroked his cock. "Have I mentioned I love you in white lace?"

She climbed up onto the table and dropped her Seeming. Her wings stretched above them. Shane watched as his personal debauched angel straddled his hips. "I'm spread. Now what?"

He thrust up. "Hungry?"

She licked her lips. "Oh yeah."

Akane surprised him. She turned on the table, straddling his head and presenting him with her lace-covered pussy. When her mouth once more engulfed his cock Shane was more than willing to provide what she wanted.

He licked around the edges of the lace. He pulled it aside, revealing the wet lips of her pussy. He thrust his tongue into her sweetness, enjoying the moans around his cock.

He needed to get the panties off of her. He couldn't enjoy her properly with them in the way, but he didn't want Akane destroying them the way she had the last pair. He began tugging them off of her, grateful when she lifted and twisted enough for him to take them off. He tossed them on the floor and pulled her back down to him, eager to sample her again.

Akane was making it damn hard to concentrate on what he was doing. The feel of her hot mouth on his cock was killing him. He was going to blow soon, and blow hard.

He wanted to do it inside her. He wanted to give her his seed, his life, his all. "Akane."

"Hmm?"

That hum around him had him arching off the table. It was definitely time to fuck his mate. "Turn around. Ride me, *a ghrà*. Make us come."

Akane turned and straddled him. A smile on her face, she lowered herself onto him, those sharp claws of hers digging into the wood of his worktable, scarring it further. Her wings fluttered above them as she sank down, pulling him into her balls deep. Akane rotated her hips and moaned. "Oh gods."

Shane went to grab her hips, help her ride him, but Akane moved, holding his hands down. She pushed them until they were above his head. He let her do it, wondering what his dragon was up to.

"Uh uh uh. Naughty Shane. You got caught fucking around, and now you have to pay the dragon."

Shane decided to play around. "But she tasted so sweet."

Akane's hips moved. "Did she?"

"Mm-hmm. I'm dying to taste her again." He thrust up into her, chuckling when she gasped. "She tasted like hot, sweet cinnamon."

Her eyes glowed. Dragon fire lit her skin from within. Her wings were golden, flaming glory above them. She rolled her hips again, and Shane bucked beneath her. Her lips curled up in a feminine smile. "Maybe you'll get a chance to taste her again."

He planned on it.

Akane began to ride her mate. She was leaning over him, pinning his wrists to the table, her breasts threatening to spill out of her bra. Her hair hung down, brushing Shane's cheeks with each stroke. The curls at the base of his cock brushed against her clit, teasing her, tantalizing her.

She couldn't wait to see his reaction to the white garter belt and stockings. She had the feeling he'd go insane when she wore them for him.

Shane thrust into her, distracting her from her thoughts. She wrapped her fingers around his wrists, pinning down her prey while she took what she wanted from him. His velvety hard cock slid inside her over and over again, dragging her closer and closer to orgasm.

He shifted, and she realized he'd planted his feet on the table. It gave him the leverage he needed to truly thrust into her. "Hurry."

From the strain on his face he was close. Akane lifted his

hands to her horns, ready to give in, ready to come with him.

Shane stroked her just right. One hand slipped down her body to pet her lace-covered breasts. The other stroked the tips of her horns. Her body quivered as their movements became jerky. They were both so close she could taste it.

Shane was panting. He was fucking her so hard she could hear the loud slap of their bodies.

Then Shane flicked the tip of her horn over and over again, sending her screaming over the edge. Her wings ignited at the force of the orgasm, the glow lighting the room behind her.

Shane yelled, his lights dancing around them, sparks landing on her skin as his Sidhe half once more Claimed her. He came, following her into ecstasy as she watched, still reeling from the strength of her own orgasm.

Finally it was over. Akane collapsed on top of Shane, the sound her gasps joining his.

"We need to buy more white lace."

She began to laugh.

"I'm serious." She could hear the humor in his voice, but was too tired to lift her head from his shoulder. "I know someone who can make an entire gown out of the stuff."

"We'd never leave the bedroom."

He tilted her head up. "Your point?"

"I have to go."

Shane paused, his hand still on his zipper. They'd gotten dressed much more quickly than he would have liked, but she was right. She had a job to do, and he'd delayed her longer than he'd meant to. "Let me come with you."

Her brows rose. "How would we do that?"

"I can sit and have tea with Ruby and Leo while you do your fly-bys."

She rolled her eyes.

"I could ride you over there."

If he hadn't sounded so falsely innocent her mind might not have dropped right into the gutter. As it was she was getting visions of a different sort of aerial acrobatics than the ones Robin had in mind. "I'm working."

His hand hovered over the tattoo for just a second before it dropped with a sigh. "Damn. Trumped my ace." He shook his head. "Curses. Foiled again."

She ventured close and hoped he wasn't faking it. She really *did* need to boogie. "Give me a kiss before I go?"

His eyes went wide before he swooped down, capturing her mouth, laying claim to it in no uncertain terms. He released her with a sigh. "Remember your mother's warning. Be careful."

She licked her lips. How long his taste would linger there? He hoped it stayed forever. "I will."

"Promise?"

She crossed her heart. "Promise. Do me a favor and have Sal guard you while you sleep, okay? Jaden's still sleeping off whatever Duncan and Moira did to him, and I want to make sure you're safe while I'm gone."

"I will. I promise."

She gave him one last kiss before flying out the door, her dragon eager to take flight. Shane watched his mate take off and sighed. Damn. He'd known she had to obey Robin, but what was about to come would break her heart. She would know she could have prevented it. Worse, she'd understand he'd allowed it to happen. He almost stroked the tattoo, but by doing so he might cause her flight to falter or, worse, call her back. It was too late now to stop what was coming anyway. If this didn't happen the way he'd foreseen it the entire prophecy would mean nothing. He *had* to let things follow their course, or Oberon's future would be beyond grim.

Akane was going to kill him when she found out.

Heart racing, he shut the outer lights of the studio. He conveniently "forgot" to summon Sal, unwilling to risk the salamander. He couldn't allow Akane's pet to be hurt in any way. She loved that silly salamander.

Shane walked through the workspace of his studio, past the display space, and found himself standing outside the vault. It took but a moment to unlock it before he swung the door open.

Here was a treasure trove of unfinished pieces and unrealized visions, things circumstances had forced to come to naught. Precious and semi-precious stones, balls of silver and gold and the occasional bit of cold iron, anathema to any of Sidhe blood, were thrown into bins and across surfaces like discarded Tinker toys. Shane, like most with Sidhe blood, had to wear special gloves whenever he worked with iron or run the risk of serious damage. He walked past several of the unfinished statues before finding the one he sought, the one that had once more begun to dance behind his eyes after talking with Tristan. He pulled the sheet off the piece and sighed.

No. Akane was *not* going to like this one little bit. But he wasn't leaving this vision out for *her* eyes.

Shane pulled the piece out and brought it to his workbench, intent on finishing as much as possible before it was too late.

Akane flew over the Dunne estate three times before

Artistic Vision

coming in for a landing. Nothing seemed out of place. None of her senses tingled. The place seemed well defended. Leo had even shown her some of the tricks up his unique sleeves. His ability to use the land to amplify his Sidhe mind powers was amazing. No wonder he'd been able to sneak up on Kaitlynn and her guards. He'd been able to enter all of their minds, erasing his image and that of Duncan from their sight until he was past the security cameras and down in Kaitlynn's dungeon.

Then, looking a little green around the gills, Leo had shown her the spot where he'd killed the vampire Jeremy West and saved his true bond. Akane was impressed, but understood on several levels why Robin had never tried to recruit the Sidhe into the Blades. With his powers Leo was phenomenally strong, but *only* on his own land.

Add in the fact that the man had no stomach for bloodshed, and his usefulness as a Blade would be severely limited. He didn't seem to have any of the specialized skills that would keep him out of combat the way Red did, or the healing abilities of the nymphs. No, he was just a Sidhe with a little something extra, not enough for Robin to pull into the fold.

She found Robin watching over Leo, who was holding a sleeping Ruby. The human was curled up in the living room on a red velvet sofa in front of the fireplace. The way Leo's face softened as he gazed at his sleeping bondmate, tender yet fierce, reminded Akane of the way Shane had looked at her. That same expression had adorned Shane's face more than once when he watched Akane, but she hadn't wanted to admit to herself that it was there, let alone what it could mean.

The truly scary part was the way Robin watched Ruby with that same look. Was the Hob in love with Leo's mate?

Robin nodded in welcome, the tender expression smoothing out to his normal, cheerful look. "She's as safe as we can make her."

"What about Shane?" Leo's voice was soft in deference to his sleeping bondmate.

Akane shrugged, but something deep inside her squirmed. She wasn't entirely comfortable being away from Shane. "Sal and your father are standing guard."

"Dad has to sleep sometimes. He's running the farm and guarding Shane. He's going to run out of juice soon."

Akane sighed. "We can call for reinforcements if you like, but if we do that we're less likely to draw the Malmaynes out of hiding." She fingered the puzzle box in her coat pocket and wished she could bring it out to play with. She needed to remain vigilant, but the golden toy called to her, *Solve me, Akane! Solve me!*

She was going to kill Shane. He should have known better than to give a dragon a puzzle. Her fingers stroked over it again, feeling the lines and grooves of its carving. She'd never hand the puzzle box over to anyone else, even after she solved it.

"And your father has declared his desire to see this war ended." Robin leaned his head back against his seat. If Akane didn't know better she'd swear the Hob was weary, but Robin was like the fucking Energizer bunny. He kept going and going until whatever needed doing was done.

"I can't help thinking that they're not going to make a move until they're good and ready." Leo stroked his wife's hair, careful not to wake her. "We have to keep her safe."

"I gather, since Kaitlynn's scheme didn't work, that Ruby was unwilling to share?" A Sidhe lord could take a second spouse despite a bond, but only if his bondmate agreed. Otherwise the bond itself would protect the Sidhe, preventing anyone from touching him or her by gifting the offender with nasty shocks that increased in intensity until the offender gave up or passed out. Akane remembered one instance where the would-be spouse persisted to the point where the shocks had resulted in death.

"Even if she had agreed I wouldn't have. They tortured her to get my compliance. Kaitlynn used her powers to make Ruby experience electrocution over and over again." He shuddered. "No matter what else happens I'll never give a child of mine to the Malmaynes."

Robin froze. "What did you say?"

Leo frowned. "I'll never give a child of mine to the Malmaynes."

Robin and Akane exchanged looks. "Could it be that simple?"

"The child would be half human. They might think it would be easy to control." Akane began to pace. "But I thought they wanted to use Leo's seed to create their own child, one as close to Sidhe as possible."

"When life hands you lemons, make lemonade?" Robin rubbed his eyes. "All of this could be ghost chasing. We know they want to control the prophecy, but do they even understand what it means?"

Akane bit her lip and hoped Shane wouldn't have a hissy fit. "It could have something to do with the statues Shane created." Leo was listening to every word they said, the frown still on his face as he stroked his sleeping mate. "The ones about you and Oberon?"

Robin shook his head even as Akane nodded. Robin stood fast as lightning, his pretty blue eyes burning bright green. "What do you know?"

"Just that the statues *do* have something to do with the prophecy, but Shane wasn't sure how."

Robin took a deep breath. "I need to speak to Shane." A miniature tornado whirled around the Hob and he was gone, the only sign of his presence the cooling cup of tea he'd left behind.

"Do you think the prophecy has to do with Robin's statue or Oberon's?"

"Oberon's." She was almost positive. Shane had finished Robin's, but hadn't quite finished Oberon's. The time for him to do so was coming.

She stood and began to pace, her fingers twitching. She had the urge to fly, to check on Shane, but Robin had given her a task and she had to complete it. She had to protect Leo and Ruby. Besides, Robin himself had gone to speak to Shane. If something were wrong, Robin would take care of it.

She danced her fingers along golden swirls. Robin would take care of Shane. She had to trust in that.

Shane could hear them moving around. Not even his father would be able to stop what was about to happen; the one who'd come for him had been too careful. Shane winced and ran his hand down the cold iron blade. He watched the blood well through haunted eyes. If he could avoid this, dear gods he would, but there was no other way.

Shane flung out his hand and allowed his blood to paint the story he wanted to tell.

"Shane."

Shane turned. Behind him stood someone he'd thought he was familiar with, someone he could trust. The betrayal was shattering. He must have planned this from the start. When the first blow came he tried to block it, but there was no stopping what was coming, no way to save him. He fought enough that they wouldn't think he'd given in, but not enough to cause himself permanent damage. He made sure both of them bled, adding their essence to the canvas he'd be leaving behind.

The blow to the back of his head sent him hurtling into darkness.

Robin stared at the wreckage of Shane Joloun Dunne's workshop and snarled. Blood, too much blood, tinted the concrete floor. Not all of it was the hybrid's, but enough that Robin would have to keep Akane from entering the room. If the dragoness scented her mate's blood splattered around the room she would go feral, uncontrollable until her mate was found and returned safely to her side.

Woe unto those who had harmed him, for dragons were fierce when it came to protecting their own.

He eyed the spot where his statue had been and stilled. Where once the ball of jagged metal and glass had stood was a new statue, one that had Robin swearing in several different languages. Upon a silver table, a figure made of gold and green glass writhed in agony. Fire somehow glittered in the glass man's core, some trick of the light that, when Robin moved, disappeared from view. Dark tendrils drifted like smoke from the table and into the man's body, the sight all too familiar to Robin's eyes. The glass man's mouth was open in a silent scream, one fist clenched around a golden, thorny rose, one petal poised to fall. Beneath the figure's clenched fist rose petals littered the floor, black glass rimmed with faded gold. The figure's other hand reached for something unseen, away from the agonized face.

Over it stood a figure in black, robed and hooded, like all cheesy villains were. But what chilled Robin to the core was the glowing green eyes in the face of the figure. Eyes he was intimately familiar with, for he saw them in his mirror every day.

Robin breathed, and the black figure shattered.

"Robin?"

He turned to find Sean Dunne standing behind him, the leprechaun's fury a match for his own. Sean was staring at the shattered black glass, his expression unreadable, but beneath his feet the earth itself heaved. If Robin hadn't been who he was he would have been knocked on his ass. As it was he almost staggered, startled anew at the strength the Dunne leprechauns showed.

"Where is my son?"

Robin allowed his claws out and grinned. "Good question."

Akane rubbed her hands up and down her arms. Something was wrong. Something was *very* wrong, and her dragon was beyond upset. It took three tries to open her inner sight, her dragon was so upset.

When she did, she cried out in horror. Shane's bright light was dimmed, barely visible to her inner eye. Blood matted his bright hair; his blue eyes were closed in what she prayed was simple sleep. She couldn't tell where he was. It was dark, even to dragon eyes. She shrieked, her song of rage loud, her Seeming falling from her in tatters, her hybrid form unleashed at the knowledge that her mate was injured, possibly dying.

"Akane?"

She turned, the rage so strong Leo seemed bathed in ruby light. "They hurt him."

"Who?" He grabbed hold of her arms, surprisingly strong for an almost full-blooded Sidhe. "Shane?"

She nodded, ripping out of his hold easily. She had to go, had to find Shane, had to stop them from hurting her mate. She needed to taste their blood, to rip into them, to feast on their pain until she was satisfied they'd never hurt Shane again.

"Akane, wait! Wait until Robin gets back, or call Jaden. Hell, get hold of Tristan if you like, but don't go alone. If the Malmaynes have Shane he might be your best bet for getting him free!"

The need to hunt, to kill was so strong she was barely earthbound. She wanted to fly, to leave this place and kill the ones who had *dared* take her mate from her. Didn't they know who she was, what she would do to them? They would lie dead before her, their carcasses rotting beneath her feet as she roared her triumph over them!

"Still thyself, Akane Russo."

She froze, the music in that voice freezing her in her tracks. If Akane was pure vengeance, then that voice promised pure destruction, the seductive song speaking to the enraged dragon within her.

Robin Goodfellow, eyes blazing with green light, stepped out from the shadows. His black nails had grown to wicked talons. She glared at him and hissed; he kept her from finding her mate, but with those glowing eyes on her she had no choice. She was rooted to the spot, unable to move as the Hob enforced his command through sheer willpower.

And then Robin did something she hadn't known was possible. Dragon song erupted from a non-dragon throat, sweet and stunning, drawing her to him with its power and majesty. Without thought she knelt at Robin's feet, purring, her head resting against the Hob's thigh in total submission to his will. If anyone could save her mate, it would be Robin.

His hand fell to her hair, stroking her, gentling her, not as a lover would but as a father, one who commanded her trust and obedience with a single glance, a muttered word. Only the knowledge that her mate was out there, alone and wounded, captured by an unknown enemy, kept the total peace he offered at bay.

"Holy fuck."

She looked up through dazed eyes to find Leo staring at her in shock. "What did you do, Robin?"

"Called the little bird to hand." Robin's hand tightened briefly in her hair before resuming her stroking. "Your brother left a disturbing statue out, but I believe he intended his mate to find it rather than I."

Leo gulped. Behind him, Ruby stirred, but Akane could barely bring herself to care. "What was it?"

The stroking stopped and Akane stopped purring. "Torture."

The dragon stirred. Her mate was hurting.

Her mate was *hurting*.

Akane hurled herself from Robin's side, the dragon's wrath once more roused. She could smell blood on Robin.

Shane's blood.

With a shriek she tore out of the mansion, uncaring that she remained in her hybrid form. Let the world think harpies had returned to plague them, because if Shane died it wouldn't be far from the truth.

"That went well." Robin sighed and rubbed his eyes wearily. Some days it just didn't pay to get out of bed. "Akane will return to the studio and find her mate's blood. She'll hunt him down, and those who have taken him from her will pay the price."

"You mean she'll kill them."

Robin turned to Leo Dunne. Sometimes the middle Dunne child seemed too innocent for what Robin feared was coming.

"Yes."

"Good." Robin blinked in surprise as Leo reached behind him. He helped Ruby to her feet, holding her close. "But there's something you should know."

"Hmm?" Robin was still processing the fact that Leo wanted someone's blood to spill.

"There are redcaps coming up the driveway, and Robin?" The fear in Leo's eyes had his little mate whimpering. "They aren't alone."

Shane opened his eyes and immediately wished he hadn't. The light from the overhead lamp damn near blinded him, the pain stabbing into his already throbbing head like dull spoons trying to gouge out his eyeballs.

"I'm sorry, Mr. Joloun. I truly am. I hope you understand that this is nothing personal."

"Sure it's not." Shane opened his eyes and stared at Mr. Klaussner, the pooka art dealer from New York. "I never got even a hint that you were Black Court."

The little man, who used to wring his hands, merely grinned. "I'm good at what I do." His eyes flashed an eerie, familiar green. "It's what I was born for."

Shane groaned. Great. Just great. Rumor had it that Robin, not exactly known for his celibacy, had fathered the rare child. It seemed Shane had accidentally met one of them. But if he was Robin's child... "Was your mother human, by any chance?"

Klaussner snorted. "As if *He* would stoop so low as to cavort with a mortal." The reverence in his voice when he spoke of Robin was undermined by the mad light in his eyes.

Shane relaxed ever so slightly. This wasn't the man he'd foreseen, then. The chances of him surviving this encounter had just gone up exponentially.

"No. My mother was pregnant with me when the Dark Queen took her, turned her." Klaussner's face rippled, his face turning almost elfin. The ginger hair on top of his head was a pale reflection of Robin's red mane. His eyes turned to pure amber rimmed with Robin's green light. Even his body changed, elongated, became lean and supple. Goat horns rose from his temples, reminding Shane of why they were often called devils. Vampiric fangs, delicate and deadly, graced his smile, a gift from his mother's change.

Oh. Oh shit. This might even be worse than the man Shane had feared it would be. "A vampiric pooka?"

Klaussner nodded, looking pleased. "She is. She's beautiful, so filled with dark power."

Shane smiled. "My mate is going to rip your head off and shit down your neck."

Klaussner merely clucked his tongue. "Speaking of your dragon mate, we know what her weakness is."

"Akane doesn't have a weakness." Shane watched as Klaussner picked up something that looked like a quilting tool his mother had. It looked remarkably like a pizza cutter, but with a hood over the blade. He thought it was called a rotary cutter, but he wasn't sure.

"Oh yes, she does." Klaussner ran the blade over Shane's stomach, sighing in pleasure as the blood welled up.

Shane held himself still, barely. He wasn't giving Klaussner the pleasure of seeing him squirm. "And that would be?"

"You." Klaussner took the blade and ran it across the dragon tattoo, making sure to cut the wings.

Shane, horrified, scrambled to pull away from the blade. *Gods, please don't let her wings be damaged.* "Why are you doing this?"

Klaussner smiled at someone standing above Shane's head. "For love."

Constance Malmayne stepped into the light, her blue-gray eyes hard, her sleek golden hair knotted at the base of her skull. She smiled at Klaussner, and suddenly Shane saw what had been missing in his visions recently. Cullen and Kaitlynn, even Charles himself, were but pawns in *Constance* Malmayne's bid for power. The vision that danced before his eyes made his blood run cold. "Does Henri know that you're planning to kill him?"

Constance smiled. "See, Hobart? I told you his visions would be useful."

Wait. *Hobart*? "Does *He* know?" Shane tried not to twitch as the blade came close to his tattoo once more. If he moved the wrong way he was terrified he'd accidentally cripple Akane. He dared not say Robin's name out loud, though he screamed it in his head. If he did say it aloud the two might outright kill him for fear of attracting the Hob's attention.

"Does who know?"

"That you're named after him."

The blade paused. "No. But He will." He looked up from the blood seeping from Shane's flesh, those familiar green eyes strange in Klaussner's thin, horned face. "I am my father's son."

The first black tentacle struck and Shane screamed, but when the poison pumped into his system the agony pushed him beyond even that.

Oh dear gods, this had better be worth it.

Akane streaked through the night sky, her wings beating furiously. Dark blood dripped from a cut across one of them, the pain a distant worry. Her wings worked and could carry her to her mate. That was all she cared about.

Akane could sense where Shane was. His blood scented the air, the sweet smell stronger the closer she got. It wouldn't be long before the others came, before Jaden made his way to his bondmate's brother, before Tristan tried to save what was left of his clan. Akane didn't care.

The Malmaynes were dead. They just didn't know it yet.

She wasn't surprised they hadn't taken Shane to the Malmayne estate. It would be too easy to figure out, too easy to check, and Jaden had proven he could get in and out at will. So taking Shane to another location was the smart thing to do.

Too bad for them they didn't know how strongly bonded she already was to her hybrid mate. Shane's scent filled her senses; his essence was etched across her soul. She'd be able to find him now no matter where in the world he went.

How could she have been so stupid? She'd finished the dragon mating yet still believed that somehow they would *not* wind up together. Shane deserved someone who could give him a normal life, not someone who would constantly put him in danger or be away from him for long periods of time. She'd known that from the start, but the gold flooding her system had ended all her resistance. She'd marked him, made him hers, and there was no taking that back. She should never have left her lover's side, never left him vulnerable. It was her fault he'd been taken, and if he died she would curl up around him and die with him.

Had he known all along that dragons *literally* mated for life?

There. She'd found him, found the source of his pain. They'd taken him to an abandoned farm, the dilapidated house and barn ghosts of what the Dunne farm was. She swooped down toward the barn, his scent strongest there. She could hear low, murmuring voices, both familiar, both surprising. It was what she didn't hear that terrified her.

Two beings breathed. Two. And neither of them was her mate.

Akane blew, fire erupting from her throat, engulfing the dry wood of the barn with her fury. Flames shot into the sky, a beacon to those who followed her.

Two figures ran out of the burning barn. Where was her mate?

Akane swooped down, her rage burning hotter than the fire behind her. On silent wings she glided, claws extended, intent on ripping, on shredding.

One of the running figures glanced back and, shrieking, shoved the other down. Akane got a glimpse of silver eyes and rumpled blonde hair. She chose to ignore the one who'd been shoved down, intent on capturing a Malmayne between her claws. She grabbed the female, making sure her claws dug into the woman's sides before beginning her ascent.

The Sidhe female screamed and struggled, but it only served to dig Akane's claws in deeper. Blood dripped down Constance's sides and legs, the wounds deep. "Let me go!"

Akane laughed. "You took my mate."

"He's still alive! He—he's in the barn!"

Akane looked, listened beneath the roaring of her flames, but no heartbeat could be detected. No breath stirred. "You lie. He's not in there." He couldn't be. If he was inside then... No. She couldn't think like that.

No heartbeat, no breath meant no life, and that was something Akane couldn't accept.

"No! Hobart's poison put him in a coma. We didn't want

him fi—fighting us."

Akane clenched her hands, ignoring the female's shrieks. "Why?"

"Transport," the female gasped. "We needed to take him away."

"To?"

"I can't say!" The female gasped as Akane loosened her grip. She grabbed hold of Akane's arms. "No! Please!"

Akane looked down. She'd taken the female high, high enough that simply letting go would be enough to kill. "Why should I let you live?"

The female was sobbing. "Please don't."

"Tell me who you were bringing him to."

"No! He'll kill me."

Akane let go.

The female screamed, barely holding on to Akane's arms. "I'll tell, I'll tell!"

Akane grabbed her again and headed toward the burning barn. "Who?"

The female told her a name that almost had Akane drop her, this time in shock.

Robin followed Leo out of the house in a foul mood. The Sidhe's odd bond with his land had at least given them a heads' up, but if Leo was correct then the man waiting for them was not one to be trifled with.

But then again, neither was Robin, and he'd danced with this one before.

"Ho, Bres." Beside him, Leo jumped. It was rare that the leader of the redcaps came from his shadowy lair. The Fomorian was one of the oldest, and last, of his kind, and ruled the redcaps with an iron fist. He'd once been king of the Tuatha Dé and forced them to act as slaves to the Fomorian rulers. Now he ruled the most brutal thugs in the fae world.

Somehow he'd wound up with the beauty of both his Fomorian father and his Tuatha Dé mother, making him one of the most exquisite-looking people to ever walk the earth. Very few could resist his charm when he chose to employ it. Even fewer wished to incur his wrath. He was vicious to those who crossed him in any way.

Robin was not impressed.

Bres, his fair head bared in the moonlight, bowed. "Ho, Pan."

Robin barely managed not to roll his eyes. It had been years since any called him that, false though it was. It was lucky for him that Pan had been amused to be associated with the Hob, finding Robin's antics entertaining. So few of the Greek gods had that sense of fun Robin so prized that he'd been honored that Pan allowed the falsehood to stand, despite Robin's objections.

To this day he lit incense in Pan's honor.

Despite the god's amusement, it wouldn't do to be pretentious. The gods, even Pan, were capricious, and had a way of making their displeasure known in fascinating, albeit painful, ways. Allowing the falsehood to stand would be bad on a molecular level. As always, Robin objected. "I prefer Hob. Robin if you're feeling friendly, but we both know you aren't, yes?"

Bres merely smiled. "Give me the boy behind you, Hob."

"That you may take him to your bitch-queen? I think not." Robin would kill Leo himself rather than subject the Sidhe to the tender mercies of Titania, even knowing sweet Ruby's life would also end. She'd want it that way, rather than a mate who'd been a plaything for the Dark Queen. The bitch always broke her toys.

Leo shuddered, and if Bres thought for one moment it was from fear he was sorely mistaken. Leo had just linked fully with the earth, using it to enhance his power a thousand-fold. The power raced through Robin's own, Leo's connection a shock and a strange pleasure to one who was also of the earth. One by one the redcaps behind Bres began to disappear, sinking down silently 'til nothing was left, not even a twitching nose. Leo had to be using his Sidhe ability to cloud the redcaps' minds, else they'd be shrieking up a storm. It explained the glazed look in the Sidhe's eyes when Robin dared glance at him.

"You know how this will end, Pan." Bres waved his hands languidly. "I'm sorry, Hob. My men have already secured the girl, and another has secured the boy's brother. Give him to me, and once we have what we wish we will fade away."

Robin watched without looking as another redcap disappeared into the earth. "My king desires otherwise."

At the mention of Oberon, Bres flinched, but it was quickly hidden. "I have no quarrel with him or you, but I must obey my queen."

Robin spread his hands, his nails curling into talons. "Then we are at an impasse."

Another redcap disappeared.

"Ruby is safe. He's bluffing. He doesn't have her."

Robin tried not to flinch as Leo's words echoed in his head. The boy was *strong* on his land; very few could breach Robin's mental barriers. He found himself more and more impressed with the Dunnes every time he played with them.

"Good. Now get out of my head."

Leo's silent chuckle echoed in his head, but Robin decided to let it pass. The boy deserved his brief moment of triumph, for things were about to get ugly.

Bres was going to attack, and he was far more dangerous than any redcap could ever hope to be.

"You fucking bitch."

The female shivered, her legs curled up as high as they could go. They were over the burning barn now, the heat blistering to Sidhe flesh. "Please don't kill me."

Akane growled and flung Constance away from the burning barn, ignoring the female's cries. Her mate *was* in the barn, unconscious, possibly dead. His scent wafted to her on the embers, fresh but subtly wrong. She let forth a keening cry, listening for an answer.

None came.

Akane entered the barn, her senses alert to any movement. She hadn't seen the male who had accompanied the female when she'd flown back down. Where he was she didn't know, nor did she care so long as he was far from her mate.

Near the back, toward what used to be the tack room, she found him. He was strapped to a table, his jaw slack, his eyes glittering in the firelight under half-closed lids. Black tendrils, ones she'd seen before, were embedded in his sides, his thighs, his arms, pumping something into him. Something vile. Akane could smell the wrongness. Whatever had poisoned her mate would leave its mark on him. She crooned to him as she yanked the tentacles away, desperately trying not to gag at the stench.

She'd seen Robin use these before to maim, to kill, but the foul, putrid odor from these tentacles smelled nothing like the poison Robin used. It was as if someone had taken Robin's essence and fouled it beyond redemption. That foulness raced through her mate's system, tainting it.

Dear gods, what if Shane changed somehow? Would the poison drag him down into the Black? Could it?

He moaned, then coughed, the smoke of the burning barn becoming thick and fierce. Akane lifted her mate from the table and raced from the barn, taking flight once they were free. She had the scents of both the female and the male. She would recognize them again. The male bore traces of Shane's blood on his claws, something he would pay for.

But first things first. Her mate was in her arms, and he lived. Akane raced to the Dunne farm and the one place he'd want to be when he awoke.

Bres struck, just as Robin thought he would, at the weakest link: Leo. Fortunately the Sidhe had come prepared, using the earth itself to protect him while he unsheathed his sword. It swayed and buckled, forcing Bres back a step.

The leader of the redcaps smiled at Leo's sword. "Cold iron doesn't work on me."

No. Robin had known that. Neither the Tuatha Dé nor the Fomorians shared the Sidhe's allergy to iron. It took something else to kill one such as Bres. The only one who had come close had been Lugh, who'd tried to poison Bres by filling three hundred wooden cows with a bitter red liquid, then "milking" them and forcing Bres to drink the liquid. Bres, under a geas to obey the rules of hospitality, had drunk the liquid, but instead of killing him it had merely forced him into a slumber so deep they'd all thought him dead. When he awoke, a thousand years had passed and Oberon, his queen Titannia by his side, was on the throne. The Tuatha Dé and the Fomorians had been nothing more than a memory, even to those whose lives were measured in centuries.

What part Bres played in Titannia's fall Robin didn't know, but some day he intended to find out.

Robin carelessly blocked a redcap, skewering it on the point of a claw before turning his attention once more to Bres. The man was attempting to take down Leo by any means necessary, ignoring the Hob as if he wasn't even there.

Well. Robin would have to fix that.

Robin smiled sweetly, and Bres tripped, almost falling on the point of Leo's sword. He flicked his hair back from his shoulders and Bres's belt broke, his pants slipping from his narrow hips. When Robin sighed, bored of the game already, Bres's sword broke.

Unfortunately, the tip flew through the air and gashed Leo's face, narrowly missing his eye. Startled, the Sidhe backed up a step and right onto the point of a redcap pike.

"Damn. Missed one." Robin muttered to himself in disbelief. How could he have missed one of the little fuckers? He reached out his hand and twisted. The redcap fell in screaming agony, his kneecap shattered.

But it was too late. Leo was on his knees, his hand pressed to the wound at his back. Bres stood over him and knocked Leo out with the butt of his sword.

Robin sighed in relief. The boy was out, and relatively safe; the last redcap was a whimpering mess, and who cared what *they* saw?

A toothy grin on his suddenly inhuman face, Robin squared off with Bres.

Now it was Robin's turn to play.

Chapter Eight

Shane stirred, moaned. Pain was etched into every cell of his body. Nausea raced through him and, barely managing to turn enough that he didn't choke, Shane puked. Thick, viscous black goo poured from his stomach, as foul tasting as it smelled.

"Ew. What the fuck is that? Tar?"

His baby sister's voice brought a weak smile to his face. He couldn't even open his eyes, but he could imagine the expression he would see there if he did. Her nose would be wrinkled in disgust, but her green eyes would be lit with worry.

"Ugh. What the hell have you been eating?" Footsteps sounded on wooden floors; Akane *hadn't* taken him to his studio. He must be in his parent's house. "Ma!" Moira bellowed, confirming it. "He's awake and he puked!"

"I remember when I used to bellow that," Shane tried to joke, but the words were barely whispered. He tried to remember what Constance and Klaussner had done to him, but he couldn't think past the pounding in his skull and behind his eyes. Pain wracked every inch of his body. "I think I was hit by a burning oil truck."

"Close enough." Warm fingers pushed back his hair, soothed him. His mate's touch burned him, warmed the cold places that had started to settle through him. "Welcome back."

He managed to open his eyes, but it was like a film had been drawn over his sight. He could barely see her, and what he did see was shrouded in shadows. "What did they do to me?"

Smoke curled from between her lips. "They hurt you."

He blinked. "I got that. What *exactly* did they do to me?"

More smoke. His dragoness was ticked. "They put things into you, pumped poison through you."

Oh. That. No wonder she was upset. Shane was in for a rough time of it, but when he told her the cure she was going to be *really* upset. He held back the shivers threatening to rip him to pieces. "I see."

Her head tilted, her expression fierce. "Do you?" She lifted him in her arms, startling him. "Strip the bed please, Moira."

Moira huffed but obeyed. Akane's tone left no room for argument, but at least she'd said please. "I'm okay, *a ghrá*."

Akane snorted. "Sure you are. You puke up black goo every day." She placed him down on cold, fresh sheets, then curled up around him. "I thought you were dead." She stroked the dragon on his arm, the tears she was desperately trying not to shed obvious in her voice.

"I know."

"You knew they were coming for you."

He nodded. He wouldn't lie to her. He couldn't. "Da?"

"He's fine. Whatever they used to knock him out didn't last long, but he is seriously pissed off." Moira took the one seat in the room that wasn't the bed and rubbed at her face wearily. "You are in *big* trouble."

"Anyone hurt?" Shane could barely stay awake. All he wanted to do was sleep in his dragon's arms.

"Leo."

His eyes snapped open at that. He struggled to sit up, but

Akane held him down. "What happened?"

"The leader of the redcaps showed up at his place to take him and Ruby to the Dark Queen."

Shane shuddered. He hadn't seen that possibility. "How badly is he injured?"

"Bres sliced him up, but he'll be all right. Mostly cuts and bruises. He managed to take out most of the redcaps by himself. Robin was seriously impressed." Akane stroked his arm, trying to calm him down.

Shane sagged back onto the bed in relief. "They shouldn't have attacked him on his own land."

"Ruby is pissed. She wants Bres's head on a pike. Apparently one of the blows came close to Leo's eye and she thinks it will leave a scar on that perfect face of his."

Shane shuddered. "He's all right?"

"Yes, Shane. He's all right. It would have been different if Robin hadn't been there, but he'll be fine."

"We owe him." He snuggled back, Akane's warmth once more driving away the strange chill, lulling him to sleep.

"Yes. We do." She kissed the nape of his neck, and he got the feeling she wasn't talking about Robin.

"*Tá grá agam duit.*"

She sighed. "What the hell does that mean?"

He smiled, unable to answer, as his sister did it for him. "It means *I love you.*"

Akane's face burrowed into his hair, her breath hot on the back of his neck as he drifted off to sleep.

"*Tá grá agam duit,* you stubborn son of a bitch."

If he'd been capable of it he would have demanded she repeat the softly whispered words, but the exhaustion wouldn't allow it. Shane let himself fall into darkness, knowing when he woke he'd have little time to hear those words again.

Akane lay beside her mate and breathed him in. Her dragon slowly calmed, but something was off. His scent *had* changed, and Akane was terrified over what it could mean.

"Moira?"

"Hmm?"

"Get Sean."

Moira nodded and left the room.

"What's wrong with him?"

Akane wasn't surprised to find Jaden had slipped into the room. The vampire would scent the change in Shane and come to investigate, especially if it involved her mate's blood the way she thought it might. "I think the poison they pumped into him is hurting him."

Jaden leaned down and sniffed, wrinkling his nose. "Let me check something." A black claw curled from where his nail had been. Jaden sliced Shane's arm, a shallow cut that should have bled a sluggish red.

What came out of Shane's body was neither sluggish nor red. Tiny black tendrils oozed out, reaching for both Akane and Jaden, a parasite eager for a new host.

"Holy fuck!" Jaden leapt back, forcing Moira, who'd returned with her father, out the door. "Don't come in."

Moira, like every other member of this crazy family, was having none of that. She tried to push past her mate, but Jaden held her fast, one eye on the ick that slithered from Shane's veins. The vampire gagged. "That is *so* fucking gross."

Akane leaned over Shane, allowing one of the tendrils close to her face. She breathed out, her flames engulfing the tendril.

An almost inaudible screech of agony raced across her senses. The tendril curled in on itself, bubbling into inanimate black goo. The remainder of the tentacles pulled back within Shane's body, writhing beneath the skin of his arm.

"Double gross." Jaden allowed Moira in, ignoring the smack to his stomach. Sean raced toward his son, growling at Jaden when the vampire pulled him up short. "You don't want to do that."

"That's my son." The ground outside the farmhouse rumbled, a sure sign of Sean's displeasure with his son-in-law.

"Listen to me. Whatever's inside Shane is dangerous." Jaden eyed Akane. "How fireproof is your mate?"

She blinked. He could not be suggesting what she thought he was.

His brows rose. "If he's truly your mate, he'll be safe, but the...thing should be fricassee. Think about it."

Once again her dragon nature took over. She found herself crouched protectively over her mate, growling at the vampire. Her wings, which she hadn't consciously unfurled, fluttered in a dominance display that would have sent another dragon either running for the hills or accepting the obvious challenge.

Jaden threw his hands up in the air. "Well, I sure as hell ain't sucking it out." He shuddered. "There's no amount of Listerine or blowjobs in the world that could convince me to do that."

She hissed at him. He wanted her to set her mate on fire or somehow drain his blood? Was he insane?

"It could work." Moira leaned against Jaden, smiling slightly when his arm went around her waist. "Aren't dragon mates immune to their mate's flames?" Moira looked at her expectantly.

"I'm not a full dragon, remember? I'm a hybrid. For all I know I'll accidentally barbecue him."

Sean leaned close and grabbed something off of Shane's nightstand. It was only when he pressed a button that she realized it was Shane's cell phone. Sean's eyes never left hers as he called the one person she should have thought of. "Is this the Seer?"

Akane bit her lip, hoping her mother had the answer they were seeking.

Apparently she did. Sean didn't even get to asking his question before her mother's quiet voice began speaking. Sean paled, but his gaze was glued to his son's body.

The thing Shane had been injected with was moving under his skin, not just in his arm but in his abdomen, his thighs, even his face. They could all see it writhing like worms under his skin. Akane grew worried as his skin began to take on an unusual pallor. His bright hair darkened, turned copper. "He's changing."

Sean hung up the phone and turned to Jaden. "Take him into the yard. Please."

Jaden nodded, silent for once. He picked up Shane and followed Sean out of the house, Akane and Moira hot on their heels.

"Why is Jaden carrying him?" Moira was watching her mate with a worried expression.

Sean grimaced. "The Seer said that whatever is inside Shane can't hurt Jaden because his blood would destroy the invader. It's part of Jaden's nature."

"Oh."

"But it can still gross me the fuck out." Jaden shuddered.

Aileen gasped at the sight of Shane in Jaden's arms. The

tea she'd been pouring for Duncan splattered on the tile floor. "What are you doing?"

Sean shook his head, unable or unwilling to speak. Jaden's mouth was grim, his eyes glittering with green fire. Duncan stood and started to approach his mates, stopping when Jaden shook his head.

He obeyed when Moira gestured him closer. "Don't touch Shane."

"Why not?" Aileen tried to block their exit from the house. "What are you doing? Why is he out of bed?"

"He's got a parasite inside him, a Dark Court one. We have to burn it out." Sean gently set his mate aside and opened the back door. "The Seer says if we don't..." He shuddered, and for a moment grief dimmed the vibrancy she was so used to seeing in the leprechaun. "I want them dead." He looked at Akane and Jaden. "If I don't get them, you will."

Jaden nodded. "Damn skippy."

Akane bared her teeth and snarled.

Aileen covered her face with her hands, but followed them out onto the back porch.

Jaden took Shane to a spot where grass had once been. Sean, using his powers, had cleared away all grass and undergrowth, even digging a shallow, round pit in the ground. There would be no chance of Akane's flame damaging the house or accidentally setting off a grass fire.

Jaden set Shane's body down in the fire pit. Her mate's arms and legs were twitching, the thing under his skin controlling his movements. She prayed with all her might it hadn't wound itself through his brain.

Akane took a deep breath and prepared to burn the affliction from the man who'd claimed her heart.

"Wait!" Aileen rushed forward. "What if he needs to be Bonded before he's immune to your fire?"

Akane blinked. "We test it." She stepped around Aileen, grateful her partner trusted her enough to let her do what she was about to do. He lifted Shane's shirt out of the way and moved before Akane blew. Flames danced across Shane's stomach. She dared not flame his hands. Those beautiful hands had to remain unscarred. A barely audible shriek made her flinch, but it didn't come from Shane. Where her flame touched his flesh it turned pink once more, the pallor that had taken over the rest of his body disappearing under fire. She nodded, satisfied and curiously aroused at the thought of bathing her mate in her flame. "Strip him, Jade, then stand back."

Jaden made quick work of Shane's clothes, those lethal vampire claws tearing the cloth in a frenzy almost too quick to see. Everyone else obeyed, moving away from the circle of earth Sean had created to cradle his son. Akane crooned to her mate, her song hopefully soothing him. When Jaden stepped back and nodded, she spread her wings and let her inner flame fly.

He ran, trying to outrace the darkness that chased him, but everywhere he turned, every door he opened only led to more darkness. Soon he would have nowhere left to turn, no place to hide. The darkness wanted to devour him, use him for its own ends, make him like...like... He flinched, the thoughts whispering to him from the darkness too evil to contemplate.

It wanted him to bow down, to succumb. To become one with it.

Shane would rather die than do what the darkness wanted.

Flame licked across his senses and the darkness retreated, screeching in rage.

Shane grinned. She'd figured it out, his clever mate, and

Shane would get to live another day. "Akane." He followed that glow to its source, the warmth lulling him. He centered himself in that flame, allowed it to protect him. Shane marched in step with it, pointing out all the places the darkness had tried to hide. The flames obeyed his wishes, destroying the invader, eliminating every trace of the darkness within him.

Shane was finally warm again, oh so warm. He basked in it like a cat in the sun, stretching beneath a heat that smelled strongly of his fiancée. He moaned as the heat licked across his inner thigh, danced across his cock with light, teasing touches. The only bad spot was a constant itch across his arm, the last bit of the darkness trying to escape the purifying fire. Shane opened his eyes to see Akane standing over him in all her glory, fire dancing across her skin, licking at her breasts. Her hair danced in the breeze stirred by the heat of the flames. Her wings were spread wide, the delicate tracery of veins glowing with her inner fire.

She was so beautiful his heart stopped. He must have been a very good boy in a previous life to have earned her love.

Shane stood and immediately grabbed his arm. The pain there was intense, the fire he'd been basking in missing. The cold was a burning pain. From a shallow cut on his arm black ooze gushed forth, the last of the darkness trying to escape its fate.

The darkness gathered itself and leapt for Akane, landing on her stomach and began trying to claw its way in. Akane hissed and batted at it, but it clung to her fingers. She breathed at it, but it dodged her flames, no longer shackled by skin and bone.

When it leapt for her beautiful, vulnerable eyes, Shane lost it. No one, *nothing* would take his mate from him.

No one.

Artistic Vision

A strange roaring sound filled the air as Akane tried to bat away the black goo reaching for her eyes. The ground beneath her feet began to tremble. There was a faint, feminine gasp, Jaden's throaty laughter, and Akane looked up, hoping to see what had surprised everyone.

Multicolored strands of light whipped around Shane's body in a strangely erotic, lethal dance that entranced her. Within those lights she could see Shane's visions appearing and disappearing like smoke. His Seeming had dropped, and a snarl was on his face as he glared at the black ooze.

"Oh fuck." Akane had heard of this. If anyone attempted to touch Shane in that moment they would die a grisly death, whipped to shreds by the fury of Shane's Sidhe half.

This was either going to hurt like hell or be the most sensual experiences of her existence.

Shane stalked out of the fire pit, the flames of her fire still glowing on his skin and hair. The others stepped away from her at his possessive display, all of them intimately aware of what was coming next. She resisted the urge to back up. It wouldn't do her any good if she did.

Her mate was pissed as hell, and he had decided to Bind her.

"I vow that from this day forward you shall not walk alone."

One of the whips of light darted out, decimating the darkness trying to wend its way inside her. Akane gasped at the touch of that light, her whole body on fire for her mate.

Gods above. No one had ever warned her that he would be able to bring her to the edge of orgasm with *light*.

"My strength is your protection, my heart is your shelter, and my arms are your home. I shall serve you in all of those ways that you require. I pledge to you my living and my dying, each equally in your care."

Akane could feel his power wrap around her, and she gloried in it. Her mate was strong, strong enough to tame the dragon, strong enough to banter with the Hob. The warm caress of it was like bathing in liquid gold, and she longed to lap it up.

"Yours is the name I whisper at the close of each day and the eyes into which I stare each morning."

Akane opened her eyes to see the last of the darkness fall to Shane's light and smiled. The Vow was almost complete. Now was the final step. When Shane finished the Vow his Sidhe magic would kick in, binding their life forces together for all eternity.

"I give you all that is mine to give. My heart and my soul I pledge to you." He lifted his hands to cradle her face between them. "You are my Chosen One. You are my Mate, and you are bound to me for eternity."

The bands of light surrounding them reared back, then speared into Akane's body in a rush of power so dizzying she almost fainted. She could feel the joining of their souls as Shane's magic twined around hers, completing her. The rush of power tingled along every part of her, pushing her into one of the most intense orgasms of her life. She shuddered in Shane's arms, her dragon song winging through the night sky. When he kissed her, drinking down her pleasure, it merely added fuel to the fire.

Akane rode the wave, barely hanging on to consciousness, Shane's soul and hers now forever one.

Robin watched Leo Dunne sleep and smiled. The man's wounds had been easily treated, painful but not life threatening. Bres had fled, his tail between his legs, his redcaps decimated by one man. And that man had *not* been the Hob. He almost gave in to the urge to laugh out loud at the memory of the look on Bres's face when he realized what, and *who*, had taken out every single redcap save one.

Gods above, he loved this family. Would Aileen consider adopting him? He tried to picture what it would be like to have someone so loving and overprotective of someone like him, but he couldn't seem to wrap his brain around it. No one, not even Oberon, felt the need to *protect* the Hob. At best, to most he was a carefully honed weapon.

Small arms wound around his neck from behind. Robin held perfectly still, unsure of why Ruby was choosing this moment to hug him. She rested the point of her chin in his shoulder and gently kissed his cheek. "You know, I saw something interesting tonight."

Robin's heart pounded. Dear gods, no. If Ruby had seen what he truly was, that would put paid to the rare, uncomplicated friendship the human had offered him. "Did you now?"

"Uh-huh." And she whispered into his ear *exactly* what she'd seen.

Robin closed his eyes and waited for the rejection sure to come. He'd lived through it before, many times, but never had the thought of it hurt more.

Instead of the rejection he'd anticipated, the little human pressed a soft kiss to his cheek. "You look like hammered shit. You need to get some sleep, Rob."

He drew in a breath he didn't even know he'd been holding, the relief almost dizzying. She wasn't going to send him away, protect her family from him. He was giddy with the knowledge that, for once, he could stay. "Didn't you know Robin Goodfellow never sleeps?"

She chuckled. "Yup, and pigs are going to fly out of my behind any minute now." She glanced behind her at her rear end. "Yup, aaaany minute."

He laughed softly. "Your mate is extremely lucky his is a true bond, or I'd steal you away from him." He would, too, if he didn't know pretty Ruby would wither and die without Leo Dunne. The thought sent a shaft of pain through him.

He would have loved her so well.

"No, you wouldn't." He turned to contradict her, but wound up speechless at the tender look on Ruby's face. "She's out there, waiting for you, and she's going to be everything you ever dreamed of and more."

He swallowed, unwilling to show even Ruby his vulnerable side. He reached for arrogance instead, never far from him. "Yes, she will be."

Ruby just tugged his hair. "Get some sleep before your head explodes."

He winced. She had no idea how close to the truth that simple statement was.

Shane barely managed to close the studio's outer door before Akane was on him, kissing him like she'd been starved of his touch, his taste for weeks instead of hours. Her teeth worried at his neck, drawing blood. Her purr thrummed against his skin, drawing a groan from him. Damn, he wanted her purring while she sucked on him, taking him deep inside her mouth. He wanted to feel that vibration, that absolute sound of *want* she was making right now.

"Gods, Shane." She lifted her head from his neck, her dragon eyes wide, her pupils blown. "It was like bathing in liquid gold."

Uh oh. Shane slung his new wife over his shoulder and padded to the bedroom. "Claws to yourself, woman."

She huffed out an offended breath. "You're not the one I want to rip to shreds." She reached down and cupped his ass cheeks, her talons cold against his skin but her palms warm. "I just want to eat you all up."

He repressed a shiver. His cock twitched, hard as a rock. He placed her on the bed, careful of her wings. "That can be arranged."

Shane hissed as she darted forward, her tongue enthusiastically lapping at the head of his cock. Endearments and encouragement in the Sidhe language began pouring from his lips when she finally took him inside her mouth.

Then she began to purr.

Shane couldn't stop himself. He grabbed both sides of her head and began to thrust in and out of her welcoming heat. Her fist wrapped around the base of his cock, stopping him from accidentally choking her, but otherwise she let him have his way, purring encouragement around him until his head fell back and he poured himself down her throat.

Akane leaned back and licked her lips, very much the dragon that got the gold. He had to laugh at the satisfied expression on her face. "Dare I ask, was that good for you too?"

She snorted, smoke curling from her nostrils. "Get your ass down here, Jethro."

He grinned. He loved it when she called him that. "Anything for you, Miz Akane." He lowered himself over her, forcing her onto her back. It was too soon for his cock to rise, but he was going to see to it she enjoyed herself thoroughly before he took her. He stroked one finger along her golden horns, enjoying the ways he shuddered beneath him. "Can I get you to come just by doing this?"

She turned dazed eyes up to him. "Wanna find out?"

He gripped both horns and began stroking up and down, enjoying the hard, cool feel of them between his fingers. Akane moaned and writhed under him, her hips jerking up against him. She bit her lip, her hands clutching at his ass in desperation.

Shane began to rise to the challenge. His wife wanted to get fucked, and Shane was more than willing to oblige her. He bent his mouth to hers, kissing and nipping at her fullness, loving the way her pupils dilated in sheer pleasure. The only thing his little seer was seeing was him and what he was doing to her.

Akane spread her legs, enticing him into her wet heat. She grabbed hold of his wrists, stilling his fingers on her horns. "Do it, Shane. Fuck me."

"I thought you wanted me to make you come like this?" He stroked her horns again, grinning when she gasped. "Well?"

She snarled and yanked at his hair, the sting strong enough to bring tears to his eyes. "Fuck. Me. Now."

"As you wish." Shane slid into her, his hands gripping her horns to hold her steady. Or so he told her. "I wouldn't want you to think I was trying to disobey and get you to come just by stroking them, right?"

She growled. "Stop and die, Shane."

He kissed the tip of her nose. "*Tá mo chroí istigh ionat.*"

She didn't even know what it meant, but she looked up at him with love. "*Tá mo chroí istigh ionat.*"

Shane began to move inside her, desperate now to feel her come around him. "My heart is within you," he translated. He wanted her to know exactly what he said to her, what she meant to him.

She cupped his jaw. "My heart is within you." She gasped,

shivered and came, squeezing his cock like a vise.

He kept his movements smooth, nowhere near ready to come. "A grá, mo saol."

She panted beneath him, a small smile on her lips. "A grá, mo saol."

He shuddered as the Gaelic phrase dripped effortlessly from her lips. "My love, my life."

Akane's eyes cleared. She gazed up at him, her expression fiercely possessive. "My love. My life."

Shane jerked, startled, as his orgasm tore through him, blinding him to everything but his wife's brilliant, loving gaze.

Akane held Shane as he panted, exhausted, above her. His back was slick with sweat, his hair, that beautiful red-gold hair, darkened still by his run-in with Black Court poison. Her jaw clenched, cold fury overriding everything else. Shane belonged to *her*, and someone had almost taken him. "I almost lost you."

"You didn't." He lifted his head, the weariness he'd fought to pleasure her deepening his blue eyes nearly to black. Dark circles ringed them. He'd made love to her without his Seeming, but his vibrant colors were dulled. A faint scar remained from where Jaden had first cut him, a vivid reminder of what had almost happened.

"Sleep, love." She caressed his hair, smiling when he leaned into her palm. "Rest. I'll protect you."

He smiled against her hand. "I know."

The utter confidence in his reply, the complete faith in his gaze almost undid the fury.

Almost.

"When do you go hunting?"

She blinked. "After." He tilted his head, but the yawn he'd

been fighting ever since he came broke free. "After I'm sure you've rested."

Shane kissed her gently. "I just Bound you. You should be exhausted."

She allowed her brows to rise arrogantly. She was a dragon. She could go days without sleep if she absolutely had to, but she'd pay for it by sleeping for days on end.

It was worth it, for Shane.

"Ruby was out for days when Leo Bound her. From what my parents tell me it was one of the strongest Bonding rituals they'd ever witnessed. Akane? I think ours was just as strong."

Ruby was human. Akane was not. "Our lives are one now." She could feel him inside her, his exhaustion threatening to drag her down too. "I need you to rest, Shane." She licked his chin, tasting salt and Shane. "Rest for us."

For just a split second his expression was shocked before carefully blanking once more. "Oh."

"What?"

"I just understand what something meant, that's all." He rolled off of her, leaving her cold. "Good night, *a ghrá*."

She sniffed. "You're evil." Now she was going to wonder all night what he was talking about.

"I know." He pulled her into his arms and she curled around him, kept her mate warm when exhaustion proved too much for the hybrid to hold off any longer.

Akane almost blew a raspberry, but the man had finally fallen asleep, truly asleep, for the first time since he'd been taken. She rubbed her hand up and down his side, enjoying the feel of his warm skin. He'd been so cold when she'd first found him she'd been afraid he'd never be warm again.

Akane stopped, frowning when she noticed something on

her arm. She lifted her hand and had to stifle a gasp. On her forearm was a golden spiral triskele, three joined, glittering swirls of light bound in the center by a single symbol. The center of the triskele was a dragon curled around a golden human form. The arms of the triskele rotated away from the dragon and her mate, the golden spirals glittering in the light like a Sidhe's skin. Akane smiled at the sign that her mate accepted her protection until she got a closer look at the figures.

The tiny human figure held a dagger in one hand and a shield in the other.

Akane tsk'd. Why was she not surprised? "Stubborn man."

Shane shifted against her, and Akane held her peace, afraid she'd wake her sleeping mate.

Shane woke to the knowledge that his wife was no longer in bed with him. "Damn it." He shifted, stretching before he opened his eyes. "Akane?"

Silence. His wife was gone, probably out hunting the ones who'd harmed him. He wasn't surprised. She'd been ready to hunt last night, but his exhaustion and her need to protect had overwhelmed her need to hunt. Shane slipped out of bed and headed for the shower, eager to get the dirt of the day before off his skin. He turned on the bathroom light and reached for his toothbrush. His mouth tasted like an open sewer grate. He had the feeling if he lit a match and blew he'd breath flame like his lover.

His hand froze as he got his first good look at himself. "Son of a bitch." Shane reached up and fingered his hair. He'd forgotten to slip his Seeming back on the night before, and now he was seeing the effects of the poison Klaussner had pumped into him.

"Akane's going to freak." His hair was definitely a shade or two darker than it had been, the gleaming copper tarnished. The gold dust of his skin had also darkened, shadowed by poison. He blew out a quick, shaky breath of relief when he realized his eyes had remained the same sapphire blue as always.

He started the shower, hoping against hope the last of the darkness would wash off, but no such luck. The water was disturbingly clear of fae grime. The only thing that washed away was the dirt of the circle he'd fried in and the blood that had seeped from his wound. Shane fingered the cut, grateful Akane had figured out the solution before it had been too late. If she hadn't burned out the parasite he'd be heading straight for the Black Court and a life of horror as Bres's bitch.

Still, the one thing he'd expected to happen hadn't yet. He was glad the initial ordeal was over, but if his vision had been correct then something else still needed to occur. Something painful.

Shane was still marked, but it was faint, a hint of what could have been. If Akane had delayed at all he'd be forever tainted, yearning for darkness in his soul. A daily battle within himself he could eventually lose, giving the Dark Queen access to his visions and an edge given to no other court. Access to possible futures was something the Seer made sure was either withheld completely or given to all courts equally. If the Dark Queen could have a sane seer at her command it had the potential to take the animosity between the courts and force it into open warfare.

Shane shivered, a chill racing across his skin at the thought. He upped the hot water, hoping to drive the coolness back, but the shivers intensified. Something stabbed him behind his eyes, the vision painful, eager to be built of glass, metal...and blood.

Oh. Shit.

Another vision hit, this one even more violent than the first one. Shane's back bowed, his head aching, his hands twitching. He had to bring the vision to life. He *had to*.

The vision switched, changed into a new one, and Shane realized what was going on. It had finally hit, and now Shane would have to do his best to ride it out. If things went well, the prophecy would be fulfilled. He didn't want to think about what would happen if it did not. The possibilities were endless, the visions of what could happen in the worst case scenario, torturous.

He reached out and turned off the water, knowing only one thing could warm him now. He stumbled out of the shower, the visions strong, grasping him in iron talons. He barely had the presence of mind to dry himself off before he staggered into the studio, naked and almost blind. He headed for the vault, seeing in sharp flashes what he had to create, the knowledge of what was to come etched in his mind and twitching through his body. His hands reached into bins over and over again until a pile lay on the worktable, the same table he'd first Claimed his mate on.

Shane's hands and thoughts flew, piecing together something he hoped never came to pass, because if it did Shane would have more than his own blood on his hands.

Chapter Nine

Akane sipped her hot chocolate and grinned at Duncan. "How's Jaden?"

Duncan glared at her, his gray eyes bloodshot. He shifted slightly on his seat, a look of discomfort crossing his face. "Enthusiastic." His mouth twisted into a reluctant grin. "And Shane?"

She snickered. She could guess why Duncan was sitting uncomfortably that afternoon. "Excellent."

Duncan shook his head. "You and Jaden are hunting tonight, aren't you?"

She nodded, all humor fleeing at the reminder of what was coming next. "Constance and Hobart need to be taken care of."

Duncan sighed. "At least Tristan agreed to feed us information."

"He did?" She'd been a bit distracted, but she should have been informed of this. She hadn't slept yet. Luckily she wouldn't feel the effects for a few days, after which she'd be forced to rest whether she wanted to or not.

"Yes. It seems he wants to try and save some of the clan, but he's not sure how many will be willing to follow him." He toyed with his mug, his expression bleak. "I think he's going to try and re-form the Clan within the White, with himself as the

Clan leader."

"That won't work. Glorianna would never allow that." Tristan was in no way strong enough to lead even the remnants of a clan as powerful as the Malmaynes. The loss of the clan was going to hurt the White.

"He thinks because he's acting as her agent he'll be able to persuade her. He may be right too." Duncan smiled as Moira came into the room and dropped beside him. "Good morning." He shared a sweet kiss with his wife. "How's our Blade sleeping?"

"Like a baby." Moira grinned over at Akane. "How's our artist this morning?"

"Last I checked he was snoring." Akane grimaced. "His coloring is off."

Moira tilted her head and stole a sip of Duncan's tea. "How so?"

"Everything's...darker. His skin, his hair. Everything but his eyes." His beautiful, sapphire eyes remained the same, thank the gods.

Duncan and Moira exchanged a worried look. "Maybe we should have a healer come in and look at him?" Duncan wasn't asking Akane, but she didn't mind. The bond between the Dunne siblings was strong, and Akane wouldn't have it any other way. They were the ones who would protect Shane when she wasn't there.

"Do you have one you trust?" Akane didn't. Dragons healed fairly quickly, but were incapable of healing others. She'd never needed a healer, and the times when she'd worked with Jaden, the vampire had either been uninjured or waved off her concerns. She had no idea how quickly he healed.

"Oddly enough, yes, I think I do." Duncan reached for his cell phone. "She might even be close by. Last I heard from her she was staying inland."

"Inland?" That was an odd way to phrase it.

Duncan dialed and held the phone to his ear. "She's a sea nymph."

"You're kidding. A sea nymph living *inland*?" Nymphs couldn't survive far from water, especially sea nymphs. What was the creature thinking? It would be like a dragon trying to survive without air under her wings; it just wasn't done.

"She's special." Duncan smiled. "Hello, Cassie. It's Duncan."

Akane couldn't hear Cassie's side of the conversation, but she could hear Duncan's. It didn't take the Sidhe very long to convince the nymph to come to the Dunne farm and look at Shane. "Thanks, Cassie. I owe you one." He hung up the phone and pocketed it. "She'll be here by sunset."

"She was close by, then?"

"Yeah. Last I checked she's been roaming the Midwest for about a year now."

Which mean the nymph had aged a year. Without the rejuvenating powers of the sea the nymph would slowly fade away and die like a mortal, forever cut off from her watery home. Akane could think of only one thing that would make a nymph leave the sea. "Is her mate human?"

Duncan shook his head. "It's not my tale to tell, but I can say that she has no mate or bond that ties her to the land."

Akane twitched. She could feel Shane stir inside her; he'd awakened. She opened her inner sight, startled to see the jumble his usually bright power was in. Perhaps it was a good thing Duncan had called in the nymph. "Shane's awake."

"Good. Maybe we can get him to eat something before the healer gets here." Moira got up and made herself some hot chocolate. "Gods, this stuff is bad for my hips." She sipped some, groaning in pleasure. "But what a way to get fat."

Duncan shook his head and smiled indulgently. "Drink up, sweetheart. Jaden and I will love you even when you put elephants to shame."

Akane laughed at the look on Moira's face. If the leprechaun's expression was anything to go by Duncan would be sitting funny for more reasons than one.

Akane's hand jerked, spilling lukewarm chocolate all over her. She blinked, trying to figure out why she was so unsettled. The visions dancing around her mate had taken on a sharp edge. "Shane?"

Moira hopped up and grabbed her coat. "I swear, that man gets into more trouble lately." She threw Duncan his coat without even looking.

"Shane's in trouble." Akane was out the door in the blink of an eye, barely feeling the cold on her human skin. She shifted partway, allowing her wings free, her warmer dragon body immune to the chill. She raced toward Shane's studio, her heart pounding.

Something was desperately wrong with her mate.

Akane eased the studio door open. She could scent no intruders in their den. Shane was alone. A hideous screeching sound emanated from behind the closed doors of the workroom. Shane must be working on another vision.

"Stop it!"

Shane's agonized scream had her breaking down the door to the workroom. The sight that met her eyes had her gasping in horror.

Half finished sculptures littered the room. Razor sharp metal and glass shavings were strewn around the room like discarded toys. Shane, naked and bleeding from numerous cuts, was tugging his darkened copper hair, his eyes wild. Around him his lights danced faster than Akane had ever seen before, dark, hideous visions that were slowly pushing the fae into madness.

"Shane." Akane stepped forward, ignoring the sharp debris. She crooned to her mate, letting her dragon song out, hoping to pull him back from the brink long enough to tell her what had happened.

"Akane?"

The plea in his voice nearly drove her to her knees. "I'm here."

He winced, tugging his hair once more. "Help me. I can't."

"Can't what, love?" She crept closer, intent on touching him, using her own body to calm him if need be.

"I can't stop *seeing*."

She winced. The visions were torturing him and they were not pretty. "I know, love. Touch me." She held out her hand. "Touch me and I'll free you."

He stared at her outstretched hand. "No." The strength of his voice shocked her. "I won't give you this."

Damn. He'd figured it out. She'd meant to try and steal his burden, take the visions tormenting him onto herself. Their bond was strong enough that she could do it, too. "Give them to me, Shane." She could handle them much better than he could.

He shook his head. "This is part of it." His eyes turned wild, his gaze darting all over the studio. "Blues and greens and whites. I need them." He began tossing things onto the floor once more, his visions blinding him to her presence.

Behind her twin gasps sounded as Duncan and Moira arrived. She waved her hand behind her. "Stay back."

A brief surge of relief crossed Shane's face when he caught sight of Duncan, but within seconds he was muttering once more. Then, with a shriek, he swept his arm across the worktable and turned, running for the vault.

"Shit. If he locks himself in there we'll never get him out." Moira took off after her brother, her Seeming falling from her. She now bore the same dark copper hair Shane did, but her green eyes had darkened. Swirls of light brown decorated the leprechaun's skin. "Shane! Get your ass back here!"

Duncan stepped carefully over the mess, his gaze glued to where his wife had disappeared. "He's lost in his own mind. I'm going to try and calm the storm, keep him focused on one vision. When Cassie gets here, bring her to Shane's vault."

Akane opened her mouth to argue but the ex-lord of the Malmayne clan was already gone, following Moira into the vault after her crazed brother. She saw the calm of the Sidhe glamour ripple across Shane's visions, forcing him to focus on one thing at a time.

Akane growled. She'd burned the poison from him the night before, hadn't she? So what the fuck was going on?

Shane panted, sweat pouring from his skin in a stinking river. "You'll weaken before she gets here."

Duncan, eyes unfocused, his Seeming long since dropped, nodded. "I know. Can you put some pants on, please?"

Shane snorted and took the pants his sister held out to him. He blinked as another dark vision was violently shoved aside. "When the time comes you'll need to strap me down."

"What's going on, Shane?" Moira, her hands on her hips, tapped her foot.

"We missed something during the purge, or it managed to

hide from Akane's flame." He shivered, viciously cold in a way he'd never before experienced. "It's in my mind, tapping into my visions. If it takes hold, you'll have to kill me."

Moira gasped. "Fuck no!"

"Fuck yes. I'll turn on you and head straight for the Dark Queen." He stared his sister down, ignoring the frown on her face. "Can you imagine what she'll be able to do if she can see the future, Moira?"

"She won't get you, love." Akane smiled, the expression vicious. "Where do I need to tie you down?"

Shane sagged in relief. Akane understood what needed to be done, and his Blade mate wasn't going to fight him on it. "My worktable."

"That's littered with glass! We can't tie him there!" Moira turned to Akane, ready to plead his case. "He'll be hurt if we bind him there."

Akane nodded, but her gaze never left him. "I know."

When she crooked her claw at him he stood, trusting Duncan to keep the nightmares at bay. "Trust my mate, Moira."

Moira, jaw clenched, turned away.

"Come to me, love." Akane crooned, her dragon song layered throughout her voice, a song he had no desire to resist. "Come and lie for me."

"On a bed of diamonds and gold," he whispered back, a vision of light pushing back the darkness for a brief second.

"Yes." Akane smiled and helped him on the table. "You're so taking me to Milan when this is over, you stubborn son of a bitch."

He shivered as she tied him down. "I love you."

She wiped sweat-dampened hair from his brow. "*Is tú mo ghrá.*"

He gasped. "Who taught you that phrase?" He hadn't, that was certain.

"You did." She leaned down and kissed him, sweet and strong.

"You are my love too."

Akane winked down at him. "I know."

Shane jerked as one of the visions took his breath away. All he could see was tarnished silver, darkened gray skies and a man shrieking in silent agony. His fingers twitched, tested his bonds as the urge to create tried to take hold.

A gentle silver warmth pushed the vision back and Shane's eyes cleared. He focused on the most important person in the world, refusing to blink until those gorgeous golden eyes filled his vision. "Hurry."

The dragoness nodded once, and Shane lost himself in visions once more.

Akane flew from the studio with only one thought in mind: find Constance and Hobart and kill them.

"Hey, Akane! Mind taking along a rider?"

Akane paused in her flight. "How are you out during the day?"

Jaden shrugged. "SPF three thousand, courtesy of the Hob." That green light flared in his eyes. "Can we go? I'm kind of wigging out here." He pointed toward the dipping sun. "I haven't seen that in a hundred years, ya know."

"I know." Akane shifted to her full dragon form. "Hop aboard."

"Damn. If only you'd extended that invitation before I was mated." Jaden winced and gingerly climbed onto her back. "Do you have any idea how loudly a leprechaun can screech?"

"As loud as she needs to." Akane took off once he was holding securely to her back.

"Who are we hunting?"

"I'm surprised Moira didn't tell you." Akane banked, following the line of the road toward the Malmayne estate. She wanted to start there but doubted she'd find the clan in residence. Constance had to know Akane was going to come after her.

"I'm surprised she knew I'd be able to come out in the admittedly fading sunlight." Jaden shifted slightly. "So, tell Daddy who needs their ass whipped."

Akane grinned. "Constance Malmayne and Hobart Klaussner."

"One of those names is familiar, but who was mean enough to name their kid Hobart? And how many ass-kickings did the dude need to endure?"

Akane rolled her eyes. "He's the son of the Hob and a pooka who was turned into a vampire while pregnant with him."

Silence. She loved when she was able to shut Jaden up.

Of course it never lasted very long. "How did the Hob take his sudden fatherhood?"

"Haven't told him yet." Mostly because she figured he didn't need to know about someone who was already dead.

"Ah. You don't think he'll react poorly to you killing one of his offspring?"

"I really don't give a shit."

"So when I get invited to his home for dragon burgers you'll be okay with that? What am I saying, you'll already be there."

"Hobart's the one who pumped Shane full of sludge."

"Crap. And I mean that literally." Jaden sighed. "Fine, but you're taking the heat for this one. I've had my yearly helping of pissed Hob, thank you very much."

She nodded and banked again, scenting the air. It was faint, but she could detect the scents of both Constance and Hobart. "They're not here."

"Duh. Smart people get out of the way of angry dragons, you know."

She chuckled, reluctantly amused. "That explains a lot."

He poked her left shoulder hard enough she grunted. "There. Turn left."

Akane turned, her wings adjusting to a sudden updraft. "I see it."

A dark sedan was heading down the road, the stench of the Malmaynes thick on it. Akane was tempted to just wipe out the entire clan, keep them from ever harming anyone else ever again, but Shane wouldn't approve of such a draconian measure.

Damn it.

"I spy with my little eye something that begins with D," Jaden hummed.

"Dragon food?"

"Congratulations, you win the kewpie doll."

"I'll take a pound of flesh instead." Akane swooped down on the car. Inside she could smell two of the people she was hunting, two who she might let live if they gave up the real culprits to Akane's claws and Jaden's teeth. She landed on the roof of the sedan, digging in when it swerved in a useless attempt to shake her off.

Idiots. She began ripping into the roof, tearing it off in chunks. When she had almost the whole thing open she took off again, hovering easily over the speeding vehicle. They should have known that running around in a fiberglass can wasn't going to save them from her wrath. "Where's Constance?"

Cecelia Malmayne, face paler than normal, stared up at Akane in horror. Akane easily kept pace with the racing car. "Not here."

Jaden leaned over her neck. "Hey, sweetie. Remember me?" He jumped down to the car below and grabbed hold of Henri's neck. The Sidhe slammed on the brakes, but the vampire held fast. Instead of throwing off the vampire, Henri wound up with four puncture wounds in each cheek from Jaden's claws. "Naughty naughty!"

Akane lit on the roof and blew smoke at the Sidhe female. "Where are Constance and Hobart?"

Henri stiffened, the gesture so slight that Akane would have missed it if she wasn't so focused on the pair. "I don't know who you're talking about."

Jaden leaned over and lapped up some of the blood running down Henri's cheeks. "Oh?"

"Constance is heading to New York." Cecelia was shaking, her eyes glued to the vampiric tongue running up and down her lover's cheek. "I think Hobart went with her."

"Liar," Jaden whispered. One clawed hand reached down and grabbed hold of Henri's penis, twisting it. "If you want to find out all about the transgender lifestyle you'll keep lying to me."

Henri gulped and held very, very still. "Constance is at a safe house. Hobart's with her."

"Where?" Jaden twisted and Henri cried out.

"Omaha!" Henri panted, his face a mask of pain. "They're in Omaha." His expression pleading, he turned to Akane. "Duncan will know where."

Jaden stilled. He was consulting with his bondmate. He rattled off an address that had Henri nodding in relief. "Please. Let us go. Or at least let Ceci go. I'm begging you."

Jaden looked at Akane and raised his brows. He was letting her make the call on this one.

"Have you given your oath of fealty to the White Court?"

Henri gulped. "No."

His response was so quiet Akane could barely hear it. "The Black?"

Henri nodded almost imperceptibly.

"When?"

"Does it matter?" Jaden shook his head sadly. "The Malmayne Clan has already fallen. Shit." He let Henri go, his expression full of disgust. Henri and Cecelia had done nothing that warranted Blade justice. While she and Jaden could intimidate the hell out of them in pursuit of Constance and Hobart, they couldn't touch the pair otherwise.

But they could make them hurt, make them bleed, to give up Constance and Hobart, and Akane would do just that until she got what she wanted.

"Where are the rest of your clan?"

"Some are heading for our new home, some have refused to join us and are seeking refuge in the White." Henri shivered, and with good reason. If the lord of Clan Malmayne had already given his allegiance to the Black officially then *all* members of the clan were considered Black. Glorianna would have no pity in her for them. The White Queen had dabbled in a game she wasn't equipped to play and had lost before she'd even begun, and those poor sons-of-bitches who ran to her would find little mercy.

"Go on, get out of here. But know this: you tell Constance we're coming after her and ripping your dick off will be the least of your punishments. Got it?" Jaden settled once more on Akane's back. "We're enemies now."

"We always were," Henri muttered.

"No. We weren't. You were just too blind to see it." Jaden patted Akane's neck. "Let's go."

Akane nodded. "Yes, my lord."

She left the pair gasping in their destroyed car, the Sidhe's eyes nearly popping right out of their stupid heads at her acknowledgement of Jaden as her lord. She'd never given allegiance before and wouldn't have now, if it weren't for Shane. Let them think that her presence in Jaden's clan gave them an edge with the Seer. Maybe it would keep them from trying anything else in the future.

She took off, already dreading the coming interview with the Hob. Robin was not going to like this latest development. That was one man who *really* hated to lose.

He was lost in a nightmare world of pain and degradation, the visions coming faster and faster. Unable to process them, he'd given up trying to make sense of them. Instead, he allowed them to flash before his eyes, helpless to hide from his own powers even deep within his own mind. More than a few of those visions showed what would happen to Shane if he gave in, if he allowed the sweet whisper of dark power currently coursing through him to take over, to channel his visions. It didn't take a genius to figure out who the seductive female figure whispering in his ear was.

The Dark Queen, the first *leanan Sidhe*. The first vampire.

Most vampires had forgotten the lore that their ability to seduce their victim's minds, to inject pleasure or pain, came from their Sidhe Queen's roots. So had most Sidhe. But Shane understood, whether he wanted to or not. When she'd given her soul over to the demon masquerading as a man, he'd granted her powers beyond those of any Sidhe who'd ever lived. But deep inside, she'd still been a Sidhe.

A flash of creamy breast, a burst of agonizing flame in his balls and Shane was screaming to be released. The vision flashed again, and Shane stood on a black road, watching something or someone drive away, someone he desperately needed to talk to. Then another flash, and Akane lay broken and bleeding, her wings torn, her horns twisted off her head. Her golden eyes had dulled to lifeless black.

Shane writhed in his restraints, the need to save his mate overriding everything else.

The vision whirled away to be replaced by a hospital room. A pretty woman stood over a child and smiled while pumping poison into its veins.

"We're losing him."

"Where the fuck is Cassie?"

Shane could barely hear his sister's voice, but the fear in it had another vision floating before him. Moira, chained and naked, marked by countless bruises, the personal cow of a vampire so malevolent he made the Dark Queen look like a sheepdog. The vampire's bright red hair had Shane shivering in horror.

"If his mind cracks nothing will bring him back."

The Liberty Bell rang, cracking on the third ring.

Duncan. That voice belonged to the Sidhe who'd mated his sister.

"Shane! Listen up! If you give in Akane will die. You hear me? Akane. Will. Die!"

Akane.

The visions swirled again, and before him was the vision that had driven him to first create the sculpture *Akane*. The dragoness soared, high and free, joy in every movement of her body. Shane watched her, a child held close in his arms, another trying desperately to follow his mother into the sky.

Shane held onto that vision with both hands, using it as a club to beat the others back. If he could hold on just a little bit longer, that one would come true.

But the darkness crept closer, and one of the children vanished.

Akane followed Jaden's directions to the safe house, changing once more to her human Seeming when they reached a quiet part of the city. The sun had finally set, but the humans were thick on the ground, forcing Akane to land on top of a building that looked like it might have a working fire escape.

"C'mon down." Jaden whispered to her, clinging to the side of the building like a four legged spider.

"You're funny." Akane made her way to the fire escape. "You're also paying for the taxi."

Jaden snickered, but otherwise climbed silently down the side of the building. Akane kept her own descent as quiet as possible but she didn't have the vampire's ability to silence her footfalls. Still, she was a Blade, trained by the Hob himself to use what the gods gave her. So Akane, realizing the fire escape was too damn noisy, chose to risk spreading her wings. She glided down to a dirty, stinking alley silently, wondering why she'd bothered with the fire escape in the first place. She shouldn't have made such a rookie mistake.

"Mating makes you crazy, especially when one of them is in danger."

Akane glared at the vampire.

"Oh! I have a present for you."

Akane walked out of the alley, praying nothing had stuck to the soles of her shoes. She'd hate to burn a favorite pair of Ferragamos. "What?"

He held out a plastic jar. "Just a little something for when we find Constance and Hobart."

She took the bottle and read the label. "Barbeque sauce?"

He shrugged. "You would have preferred Heinz 57?"

Akane held up the barbeque sauce and shook it. "Taxi!"

"You're no fun anymore."

The cold was seeping into his bones. The children were gone. The dragon was gone. Only the voice remained, whispering.

"Shh. I have you now."

Seagulls. Why did he hear seagulls? Waves crashed on the shore, gently washing against the bare feet of the man with the silver hair and sad eyes. Something precious had been lost in the waves and might never be found again.

Crows cawed in the distance, answering the call of their lord, but whose side he was on no one knew. Darkness followed him, and the road forked before him, one full of fog, one dark as a moonless night.

A dark-haired man sat at a bar drinking whiskey, remembering a time when he rode a destrier at the side of the lord with the silver hand. He lifted his glass in remembrance of the fallen lord.

"Shh. Duncan, I think I know what's going on."

Oh goody. At least someone had a clue.

"Can you heal him?"

Duncan sounded pretty tired. He should go take a nap.

White sheets on a white bed. Monitors blipped and a woman wept. Black nails caressed a pale nape as hope died.

"He's losing his touch with reality. The parasite was burned away, but not before planting a dormant seed. When Shane and Akane mated the seed woke and did this, but I don't think it was supposed to be triggered just yet. I'm going to root it out. Moira, I'll need the salamander in here to kill it, okay?"

He couldn't hear what else was said. A crow feasted on one bright blue eye as the farm burned around him.

"Now I need you to do one more thing for me, okay, Moira?"

Shane watched the axe fall, taking the hand of the king.

"Cover your ears."

All the visions stilled as the most beautiful voice in the world drove them back into darkness.

Akane jumped out of the cab, a shiver of dread running through her. "We don't have much time." Jaden nodded, that brash tongue silent for once. They stood before the safe house, knowing it was more than likely a trap. "I'll take the heat for killing Hobart. You take down Constance."

"She's the Black's Malmayne lord."

Akane stared at her partner. "How do you know that? I thought Henri pledged them over."

Jaden shook his head. "He lied. I could smell it on him."

One eyebrow rose. "Really?"

Jaden snorted in disgust. "It was stinky. Kinda like camel piss."

Akane blinked. She was not going to ask. She was *not*. "Are we sanctioned for this hit?"

"You have doubts?"

Jaden and Akane both flinched. "Robin."

"Did you think you could hide the signs from me of one of my own?" Black claws caressed her cheek and Akane bowed her head.

"Forgive me, lord. I only thought of my injured mate."

Those sharp-as-fuck claws tapped, drawing blood. "I know." Jaden grunted. The Hob had exacted blood price from him as well. "The kill is mine."

"Yes, sir." Akane remained bowed, waiting for Robin's permission to move.

"Take the female. Make an example of her, but leave enough recognizable that Glorianna will be satisfied with the death."

"Yes, my lord."

She didn't hear Jaden respond. For a split second she was afraid for her partner, that Robin's price had been higher for him than it had been for her.

"Rise."

Akane lifted her head, almost dizzy with relief when Jaden appeared unharmed.

"Whatever you do, stay away from the back parlor. Do you understand me?" Robin's hand pushed back her hair from her forehead like a proud papa. "I will be most displeased if you disobey." The tone of voice was quiet and pleasant, but the intent was not. Whatever Robin had in mind for his errant child was not to be witnessed by outsiders.

"Yes, my lord."

"Yes, sir." Jaden nodded once, his gaze already glued to the upper story of the safe house. Green flashed through his ebony eyes. "She's up there. Hobart is in the basement, my lord."

"I know." The Hob once more sounded amused. "Go. Exact Oberon's Justice for what was done to Shane Joloun Dunne. May the gods have mercy on her soul, for we shall not."

The Hob smiled at them, sauntered up to the door as neat as you please, turned the handle and went inside the house, for all the world as if he lived there.

"That man has diamond balls."

"You mean brass," Akane corrected. She took a deep breath and looked around, hoping the street was empty despite the early hour. But the fact that they were in a fairly nice neighborhood put paid to that hope. People were beginning to come home from work in the early evening light. She eyed the front door and considered whether or not she had the same balls her boss did.

"Nope. Diamonds are a lot harder. Besides, they're a girl's best friend."

Akane stared at her partner. "That's just wrong."

Jaden winked and began climbing up the side of the building.

"Show-off." Akane braved the front entrance but extended her claws just in case. If Constance made a break for it the punishment would be over far too quickly, but Akane couldn't risk the Sidhe female escaping. She set her foot on the first stair when a feminine cry of distress echoed down to them. Jaden had apparently made his appearance and Constance was none too happy about it.

"Hey! Leave some for me!" Akane cried out, racing up the stairs.

Tonight Constance Malmayne would die.

Akane burst into a very feminine room. Pale pastels

adorned the walls, matching floral prints on the bedspread and sheets. The furniture was a pale golden brown. A nicely padded armchair rested before a fireplace faced with white marble.

"What took you so long?" Jaden had his arm wrapped around Constance's neck, his hold just tight enough that the Sidhe female couldn't break free. He shook the woman's head. "Stop that. Only three people in my head at a time, thank you."

Akane grinned. "Let me have her."

"Are you going to do that head ripping thing? That is *so* hot."

Akane tilted her head and pretended to think about it. "Nah. I was thinking of playing butterfingers."

"Butterfingers?" Jaden frowned. "Isn't that the game you used to call bombs away?"

"Yep." Akane examined the toe of her shoe, frowning. Something dark and icky stained the point. She rubbed her shoe on the pale rose carpet to try and clean it.

"You can't kill me." Constance trembled in Jaden's hold, whether from fear or from the effort to break into the vampire's mind Akane didn't know.

"Haven't we heard this song before?" Jaden tossed her like a doll, sure Akane would catch her.

Akane grabbed hold of the flailing Sidhe. "It's an oldie but a goodie."

"You think I'm no threat to you? You think if you kill me the Malmaynes will leave the Dunnes alone? Is that it?" Constance laughed, the sound bitter. "She has plans for them, plans we were only a small part of. This is bigger than the stinking half-breed Dunnes."

Akane caressed Constance's cheek much as Robin had done hers. "Really?" She exchanged a look with Jaden, getting his approval to continue questioning Constance. "Tell me more."

Black lace over blood-red eyes. Claws ripped away the veil and revealed nothing but darkest night. Bright light dimmed in the face of tragedy. Chaos became blind in the name of love. White cloth coated in innocent blood. Rage and grief took vengeance side by side as love drained away.

The visions were coming too fast now to make much sense. Shane held on to the sweetly singing voice, his only lifeline in the maelstrom around him. Without that voice he'd already be mad, the visions driving him over the edge.

Lost. He was lost. They were lost, memory a fragile thing, easily broken. Tainted blood brushed against his tongue, poisoned his dreams. His only hope lay in the rise and fall of the fickle sea.

"There's some sort of plot against Oberon, but I don't know all the details. Just our part in it." Constance wriggled, trying to break free of Akane's hold. Just because Akane was short people continued to underestimate her. There was no way the Sidhe female was getting away.

"Which was to get the child of Dunne." Jaden gripped Constance's chin, forcing her to stare into his eyes. "I take that personally."

"The child of Dunne will one day perform an act that will change our world." Constance parroted the prophecy. "The child had to be in our control."

"So you could hand him or her over to the Dark Queen."

Constance nodded. "My father had it all planned."

Jaden barely blinked, but Akane's partner was shocked. If this went back to Cullen... "What about the original marriage contract between Duncan and Aileen?"

"That had nothing to do with the prophecy and everything to do with power. We knew Sean Dunne would marry into the Joloun family. If we had a toehold in the family we thought we might be able to influence him."

"How?"

Constance bit her lip, refusing to answer.

"Answer me!" Akane breathed pale flame on the column of Constance's neck.

The Sidhe shrieked. "How what?"

"How did you know Sean Dunne would marry into the Joloun family?"

Constance tried to protect her neck, lifting her shoulders. "The Seer."

Akane's eyes closed. Damn her mother and her policy of handing out visions. "But you didn't know it would be *Aileen* who would bond with Sean."

"Thus becoming part of the prophecy."

"Is that why Kaitlynn insisted on Leo as her sperm donor?" Jaden's claws scraped down Constance's arm, raising red welts on her pale skin.

"She wanted the Dunne with the purest Sidhe blood."

"And you? How would Hobart feel if you got Leo in your bed?"

"He understands prophecy," Constance whispered.

"Oh yeah. Every man thinks of prophecy when another man is shoving his dick in his woman." Jaden rolled his eyes. "It's sort of like England but...different."

"The child would have been ours!"

"If it wasn't for us meddling kids?" Jaden gripped

Constance's throat, ignoring her yelp of pain. "I say we kill her."

"I say we let the Hob question her."

Constance stilled. "Robin Goodfellow is here?"

The terror in her voice proved she was smarter than she seemed. "Yes. He is."

At that point the real struggle began. Constance pivoted in Jaden's grip, ignoring the long scratches that appeared from his claws. She lashed out with her foot, catching him the upper thigh. Her elbow flew back, catching Akane in the throat. Akane's grip loosened and the Sidhe was free.

"Oh goody. I was hoping for a fight." Jaden laughed and went on the attack, dancing around the Sidhe with lazy grace. His hands moved, and small cuts appeared on Constance's face. He licked his lips at the sight of the blood. "You're not getting out of here alive."

"I know." She reached up and clasped the simple onyx pendant around her neck.

Neither of them could have predicted what happened next. The explosion damn near destroyed the safe house, sending both Jaden and Akane flying. Akane unfurled her wings, halting her flight through the air. Jaden didn't fare so well. The vampire plummeted, knocked cold by something that left a bleeding gash on his forehead.

She flew down and scooped the vampire up in her arms, racing skyward in an effort not to be seen. Jaden was unconscious, unable to help. There was no sign of Constance.

She hoped the bitch had been blown to smithereens.

Akane flew over the house just to make sure and blinked. One room remained standing amidst the rubble. One room in perfect, horrific order. Akane hovered over the room and stared at the black sludge that coated the walls, the floor, every bit of furniture within. Only the ceiling was gone, the victim of the explosion. Akane wasn't sure why when not even the furniture had overturned.

Then the scent hit her, that acrid, horrible stench of the *thing* that had filled Shane's veins. Akane's flame swirled around her, her wings glowing with it. That thing needed to die before it could touch any other living being.

She blew, burning the room to ash in the blink of an eye. She didn't have to worry about someone caught in the flames. From the looks of things Robin was already gone, his job done, his erstwhile son either dead or close to it.

When she was sure none of the sludge had survived her fire, Akane took off, Jaden cradled in her arms. There was still no sign of Constance, but Akane couldn't worry about the Sidhe now. If Constance had survived, she wouldn't stay alive for long. If the Dark Queen didn't take her out for her failure to capture Leo, Akane would see to it that she died a long, lingering death by fire.

Akane headed home, already aware that Shane had been saved.

Shane blinked. The visions before him weren't swirling, twirling, puking, hurling or otherwise doing something that would make him want to do any of the above. Moira was staring down at him, her eyes red from crying. Duncan, pale and trembling, held a hand to his head.

"Hello."

Shane looked up into a face too long to be pretty, too interesting to be called plain. Her full, bow-shaped lips were curved in a smile. Her nose was slightly crooked, as if she'd broken it at some point and it hadn't quite healed right. Her eyes were absolutely huge even in her human Seeming, a turquoise so bright Shane blinked to see if they were real. Their most dazzling aspect was the intelligence and humor that lit them from within. Her forehead was really a fivehead, further elongating her face. She'd made an attempt to hide it with bangs, but then she'd pushed half of those bangs back with a headband. The ends stuck out of the back of the headband, giving her an odd, rooster-like look. She had a sharp, pointed chin and quirked, full eyebrows. Her hair in her Seeming was brown, but it would be sea green in her true form.

Shane smiled. "Hello." There she was. He'd been wondering when she would show up.

"My name's Cassie." Long fingers brushed back his hair. In the background Sal barked happily. "You gave us quite a scare."

"It was a lot less pleasant on my end." Shane's throat ached. His voice sounded weak and scratchy, like he'd been screaming. He probably had been, but he didn't remember it.

"Those were some mighty powerful visions you were having." Duncan sat wearily beside Shane's bed. His gray gaze was full of speculation. "How many of them will come to pass?"

Shane shrugged. "I have no idea."

"Well. That just sucks." Duncan ran a hand through his hair wearily. "Some of them involved Jaden and Moira."

"I know." And Shane was now on the path to ensure they never came to pass, but there were still forces out there that would try and make them come true. "Jaden's hurt."

Duncan stared at him in disbelief before sighing. "I agree with Jaden. You *are* a freaky-ass dude." He stood, his head shaking. "But you're *our* freaky-ass dude. Get some rest, okay?"

Shane nodded even though Duncan wasn't looking. "Would you look at him? He took a powerful blow to the head."

Cassie nodded. "What race is he?"

"Part vampire, part Robin Goodfellow, all pain in the ass."

She blinked, amusement once more lighting her face and turning it from plain to riveting. "Ah. That should be interesting."

Shane chuckled. "Understatement of the century. Jaden's something else." He tried to sit up, startled to find how weak he was. He could barely get his head off the pillow. "Akane will be here soon too."

Long, slender hands pushed him back down with ease. "I'll send her in as soon as she gets here, I promise."

A fragment of a vision floated before him and Shane gasped. "Who's after you?"

She froze just long enough to confirm his vision. "I don't know what you're talking about." But the warmth that had been so much a part of her was closed off now, her bearing chilly and stand-offish. She'd closed down on him, and Shane would have to be careful what he said from here on out.

"I'm sorry. I didn't mean to pry. Your business is your own." He made sure to get just the right amount of sincerity and regret in his voice. Eventually he'd see exactly what he needed to see. It would come to him in time.

His part in this was almost over.

She thawed a bit, smiling at him once more. "Thank you. Now rest! Or you'll undo all the hard work I just did."

Shane allowed himself to do just that, drifting off to the sound of a softly sung lullaby.

Akane landed in front of the Dunne house. She took just enough time to hand over the still-unconscious Jaden to his two mates before rushing off to Shane's studio. She didn't care that she could feel him deep inside, knew he was all right. She had to see it with her own eyes.

She slammed into the studio at full tilt, only stopping long enough to shut the door to the cold. She raced into his small bedroom and sagged in relief.

Her big man was curled up on his side, one hand under his cheek. The other clutched the puzzle box he'd given her for her birthday. Akane smiled at the sight. She opened her inner vision to check him with that, just in case they'd missed anything again.

Something inside the puzzle box gleamed, glittering like a gem. Akane narrowed her eyes and did her best to ignore it, but the damn thing kept calling to her sight. "What the hell. Why not."

She went to the bed and gently lowered herself onto it. She took the puzzle box from his hand, glad her action hadn't awakened him. She studied the golden box once more.

Damn, her mate did fine work. She recognized several of the symbols he'd carved into the box, like the...wait. Wasn't that the tattoo that had appeared on her arm? She glared at him for a split second before realizing exactly how futile it was to be pissed over it. The man had a good idea she was eventually going to accept the mating. Her dragon half and his Sidhe half would have ensured it no matter how desperately she tried to get away.

Still. There were times when he was a seriously freaky dude. "We are going to have the weirdest children." She brushed her hand against his back, smiling at the warm strength of him.

Akane turned her attention back to the puzzle box. It wouldn't take her long to figure out how to open it. How difficult could it be?

Epilogue

Three weeks later...

Robin stared at the completed statue of Oberon. A female figure rose from the waves, her upper body the only part of her visible. She reached for Oberon, their fingertips touching, a look of such pure yearning on her face that even Robin was moved.

Shane had completed Oberon's art piece. What had Robin missed? He shook his head, once more amazed at the talent that seemed to run rampant in the Dunne family. Turning, ready to leave the studio, he paused. Under the pedestal was something draped in black cloth. Curious, he lifted the cloth off the figure.

Robin hissed. There, done in nearly black glass, was Oberon's face. His *fanged* face.

He dropped the cloth back over his king's head and left the studio. Something was going on, and Robin needed to find out what. First thing to do would be talk to Shane, find out what the hybrid had seen and, more importantly, which vision would come to pass.

"I hate you! What is this thing, a portal to Hell?" A golden puzzle box went flying past Robin's head, followed swiftly by one fast-moving hybrid with bright reddish-gold hair and laughing blue eyes. "Oberon's crown should be this well guarded, you, you—JETHRO! Get your ass back in here!"

Shane Joloun Dunne popped his ass onto the banister of the Dunne farmhouse and grinned at the Hob. "Evening, Robin."

Robin nodded. He had to visit more often. These people entertained the hell out of him. "Good evening, Shane. How is your mate enjoying her present?"

"Oh, she likes it just fine." Shane leaned back against the post and stretched his long legs out in front of him. "I think it's the pregnancy that's making her insane."

Robin stilled. "Pregnancy?"

Shane nodded, his expression wicked. "Twins."

"Congratulations." Had the prophecy been fulfilled? Was it Shane's child who would be the child of Dunne? "Wait. Does *she* know she's pregnant?"

Shane chuckled, but didn't answer.

A sea nymph stepped around the corner of the big Dunne house, her mousy brown hair pulled back in a ponytail that did little for her long face. She was a gangly thing too, tall and lean, with big wary eyes that stared at him in something akin to horror. She was dragging a suitcase behind her. "Oops. Sorry."

"Hey, Cassie. You heading out?"

The way Shane spoke to the woman let Robin know she was an honored guest. Robin relaxed ever so slightly. This must be the woman who had healed Shane. Robin had yet to meet her. He'd been summoned back to Oberon's side to give him an update on the Malmaynes.

Oberon had not been pleased to learn that they'd lost the clan before Robin had even started his investigation. He'd extended an invitation to all the Malmaynes who wished to avoid the Black Court, hoping at least some of them would take him up on it and give their allegiance to the Gray. So far, a small contingent had come forth, led surprisingly by Tristan Malmayne. Oberon was waiting to see if any more of them would follow the young Lord.

Robin wasn't going to hold his breath.

Robin stilled. There was an ornate pearl ring he recognized on the woman's hand. A surprising development indeed, even in such a surprising family. He studied her, looking for signs of her parents in her odd, almost homely face. "You are far from home."

"So are you."

Robin allowed his brows to rise, challenging her to say more. He found himself further intrigued when her spine straightened and she stared at him head-on.

"You know where you're going?" Shane stood up and helped Cassie put her bag in her car.

"Yup. Out to the road, make a left, head straight on through the rest of Nebraska until I hit Utah and eventually Colorado." She held out a piece of paper. "Are you sure I'll be able to hole up here for a while?"

Robin stared at the paper over Shane's shoulder, shamelessly eavesdropping. He stared in shock at his own address. He met the hybrid's eyes, his own narrowed in suspicion. Shane was up to something.

Shane *winked* at him. Winked, like this was nothing but one of Robin's own pranks. "Yup. Trust me, they'll be delighted to have you."

"Are you sure?"

Shane grinned. "I checked with the owners."

Did he now? Odd, Robin couldn't recall that conversation.

"Just remember, the owners work for the palace, so stay away when you hear the King is coming to visit."

She shuddered. "You gotcha. I have no desire to meet a royal."

Now *that* was even more intriguing.

"Thanks, Shane." The nymph hugged the hybrid, her expression full of gratitude. "I mean it. I don't know what I would have done without you and your folks."

"You would have survived." Akane stepped out from around the house and wrapped her arms around her mate. The puzzle box was in her hand. It looked exactly like it had the day Robin had first seen it. "You're strong."

The female, Cassie, shrugged. She looked oddly embarrassed. "Yeah, well." She turned and stared at the road before giving them both a quick hug. "I'm outta here." She gave Robin a brief, formal nod. "Nice to meet you, my lord."

"Cassie, wait!"

Robin turned swiftly. Ruby Dunne had dashed out of the house like a madwoman. She threw herself into Cassie's arms and hugged her tight. "You visit us, you hear?"

Cassie hugged back, and her expression set Robin back a step. This was a woman starved for affection, and Ruby was handing it out to her in super-size quantities. "I will, Ruby. You have my word."

Well now, this was a fascinating twist, wasn't it? He watched as the nymph, waving good-bye, took off down the wintery road toward whatever fate Shane Dunne had seen for her. She wasn't the prettiest lass he'd ever seen, but there was something about her face that caught at him. Could it be? "Is she mine?"

Shane shook her head. "Nope." He put his hand on Robin's shoulder. "You'll meet yours before she meets hers, but she'll see hers before you see yours."

Robin blinked slowly. What the hell? "Care to explain yourself?"

Shane gave him a shit-eating grin. "Let's just say the child of Dunne has just done his duty." And Shane took his laughing mate back into the Dunne house, leaving Robin standing out in the cold, confused as hell—and more curious than he could ever remember being.

A small hand patted him on the head. "You'll get used to it." Ruby Dunne took his hand and pulled him into the warmth and the light. Into something he longed for with all his ancient, weary heart.

Home.

About the Author

Dana Marie Bell wrote her first short story when she was thirteen years old. She attended the High School for Creative and Performing Arts for creative writing, where freedom of expression was the order of the day. When her parents moved out of the city and placed her in a Catholic high school for her senior year, she tried desperately to get away, but the nuns held fast, and she graduated with honors despite herself.

Dana has lived primarily in the Northeast (Pennsylvania, New Jersey and Delaware, to be precise), with a brief stint on the U.S. Virgin Island of St. Croix. She lives with her soul mate and husband Dusty, their two maniacal children, an evil, ice-cream stealing cat and a bull terrier that thinks it's a Pekinese.

You can learn more about Dana at www.danamariebell.com or contact her at danamariebell@gmail.com.

www.samhainpublishing.com

Green for the planet.
Great for your wallet.

It's all about the story...

Romance

HORROR

Retro ROMANCE

www.samhainpublishing.com

CPSIA information can be obtained at www.ICGtesting.com
Printed in the USA
LVOW13s1056250813

349523LV00002B/226/P